Dreaming of Gwen Stefani

Dreaming of Gwen Stefani

Evan Mandery

BROOKLYN, NEW YORK

Printed in Colombia
First edition
10 9 8 7 6 5 4 3 2 1

Library of Congress Cataloging-in-Publication Data
Mandery, Evan J.
  Dreaming of Gwen Stefani / Evan Mandery.
     p. cm.
  ISBN-13: 978-0-9771972-6-2
  ISBN-10: 0-9771972-6-3
  1. College dropouts--Fiction. 2. Cookery (Frankfurters)--Fiction.
3. Stefani,
Gwen, 1969---Fiction. I. Title.
  PS3613.A536D74 2007
  813'.6--dc22
                         2006033942

For my grandparents, Be and Matty

FIRST STANZA

Into her grove went the fair Kamala,
At the entrance to the grove stood the brown Samana
As he saw the lotus flower,
Deeply he bowed.
Smiling, acknowledged Kamala,
Better, thought the young Samana,
To make sacrifices to the fair Kamala
Than to offer sacrifices to the gods.

— *Siddartha*, Herman Hesse

Papaya has natural digestive properties.
— United States Department of Agriculture

1.

Someday I will tell her the story of how I found her. We will lie in bed together on a rainy Sunday morning and I will tell her the whole thing. She will laugh since it could not have begun more innocently.

I will tell her how it happened on Easter afternoon, Violet off at her mother's for dinner. Violet knew better than to ask me to go. It would have been more than I could bear. She left me instead to spend the day lounging on the couch. I had a turkey TV dinner in the oven, the one with the cherry cobbler, and the television remote in my right hand, all the makings of a perfect holiday. I flipped through the channels aimlessly, searching, always searching.

I cared little for popular music. I had never even heard of VH1—Video Hits One—though I had passed it by many times. Juvenile nonsense. Twaddle for the masses.

And then I saw her.

She danced and kicked across the stage, her life force exploding, energy incarnate. I heard the voice for the first time, the brooding ululation that suggested that this person was more than a pop star, that this was a person of great substance. I will tell her that the song was "Spiderwebs":

And now I'm stuck in the web
You're spinning
You've got me for your prey

She will laugh at the irony.

I will tell her how I paused and watched, watched the entire hour of *No Doubt: Behind the Music.* I will tell her how I became absorbed in the suffering of the band—in the suicide of its original lead singer, the years of perseverance without recognition, the wonder of whether the sacrifice had all been for nothing. I will tell her that I could not turn away from the tale of her own struggle and heartache, broken up with after six years by the bass player in the band, the only man she had ever loved, the man she thought she would marry. I will tell her how it riveted me to hear how that pain worked its way into her music, ultimately strengthening her and her band, still together despite it all.

I will tell her how I ran to my journal and wrote for hours on end about the incredible being I had just encountered. How fortunate I considered myself to coexist in the same time period. We wander through life searching, searching far and wide for something we cannot even name. What is it? A kindred spirit? A sympathetic life force? A soul mate?

Whatever it is, I had found it. On television of all places. The improbability of it staggered. What if Violet had persuaded me to go to her mother's? What if I had not been watching that station at that moment? *Shane* was on Bravo at the same time. It could just as easily have been Jack Palance I found. So many variables. So many forces that needed to conspire to produce this most unlikely result. But they had. The fates had deemed it worthy.

I found it. I found her.

I will tell her. I will tell her all of it.

And she will understand.

2.

"Two with mustard and sauerkraut."

Mortimer Taylor Coleridge moved by instinct, an efficient, finely tuned machine. His right hand reached for the buns--down and to the right into the warmer that kept the bread crisp. Then he flipped the roll end over end from one hand to the other, his signature move. As he did this, he speared a frankfurter with the tongs. He swept the hot dog aboard the bread with a flourish, then another. Two loaded, ready to be dressed.

He kept the franks in his left hand as he moved to the condiments, one between his thumb and forefinger, the other between the ring and middle fingers. He could hold four in one hand at a time, eight in total, the practiced result of years of stretching. Here some of the servers would switch hands, moving the franks from the right hand to the left so they could apply the toppings with their dominant hand. To Mortimer, this was wasted effort. Switching hands took half a second, more if multiple hot dogs were involved. Over the course of an hour this unnecessary movement reduced output by as much as ten frankfurters, an efficiency loss of at least three percent. Mortimer scorned the step. He had achieved complete ambidexterity, and could perform all of his serving functions equally well with either hand. He smeared the mustard, spooned on the sauerkraut and set the dressed hot dogs on the counter.

"One dollar fifty."

The customer did not have his money ready; they rarely did. They did not share Mortimer's concern for efficiency. They did not, as Mortimer did, have their keys ready before they reached their front door, nor did they walk out in the morning with four pennies in their pocket to ensure that they would not receive one-cent pieces in return for any of the day's purchases, as Mortimer did, nor did they walk hypotenuses across avenues to save distance crossing streets, as Mortimer did.

Here at the Papaya Queen, they had efficiency forced upon them. When the customer finally produced his payment, he found the change already waiting for him: two quarters handed to him as the dollars are taken from his hand, every step of the transaction anticipated. Perhaps the customers had time to waste. Mortimer Coleridge did not.

Another patron stepped forward. "One with mustard, one plain, one with mustard and sauerkraut," he said.

"Fifteen," Mortimer thought to himself. There were twenty-six distinct ways to order three hot dogs, from three plain to three with mustard and sauerkraut to all of the more complicated combinations in between, like one with mustard, one with sauerkraut, and one with mustard and sauerkraut. The math could get a little tricky. Some people fell into the trap of thinking the number should be sixty-four. Each dog could be dressed in one of four ways—with mustard, sauerkraut, both, or neither—just cube four and you had your answer, the reasoning went. But this ignored repetition. It did not matter whether someone ordered hot dog one with mustard and the others plain or hot dog three with mustard and the others plain; this was still an order of two plain, one with mustard.

"It's the difference between combinations and permutations," Mortimer had explained to his colleague Garcia on several occasions, though Garcia never seemed to grasp it. It was easier to see if you wrote it all out on paper, which Mortimer Coleridge had done. Not only did he write them all out, he assigned a single number to each of the different combinations and committed them all to memory. Thus when someone placed an order for three hot dogs, as this customer just had, Mortimer did not have to struggle to remember the specifics of the order, only the number he had pre-assigned to the combination. One plain, one with mustard, and one with mustard and sauerkraut had been designated as number fifteen.

As he went through the order, Mortimer mouthed the shorthand notation to himself. "No, no," he muttered as he placed the first frankfurter directly on the counter. "Yes, no," as he smeared mustard but not sauerkraut on the second (mustard always came first in his system). "Yes, yes," as he treated the third. The customer stared at the counterman's peculiar behavior, but Mortimer did not feel his gaze. He was too absorbed in his work.

All the same, the customer continued to gawk. Mortimer Taylor Coleridge did not look the part of a hot dog counterman. The customer could not say what he did look like precisely, but whatever it was, it was surely not a frankfurter vendor. He had a disturbing appearance. His eyebrows and mustache were unnaturally thick, and furled his face into a perpetual frown. His skin was tough and leathery, strange for a man who spent even the brightest of days manning a frankfurter grill. Perhaps, the customer thought to himself, the hot dogs emitted some toxic fume that prematurely aged skin. And then on the right cheek the feature from which the customer could not draw away his eyes: a massive black ingrown hair, burrowing under the hot dog man's face, pushing the surrounding skin upward and outward, a giant blotch on his countenance, overwhelming all of its other features.

Strangely, the hot dog man was well groomed. More accurately, he had made considerable efforts to groom himself; whether they had been successful or not was another story. He had matted down his hair with gel—too much really, it captured the fat that wafted through the air of the store. Over the course of the day, the grease and gel coalesced, which made his hair glisten under the lights.

He had the styling gel on his mustache also, where it obviously had been applied with great care as well. Perhaps it looked good when he left his apartment in the morning. Perhaps he did not know that as the day waned that the mustache too became speckled with globules of lard.

He wore a button-down shirt, another peculiar juxtaposition. The shirt had also been treated with great care, starched and pressed so that the collar held its shape as if it were new. It had been treated with the sort of attention ordinarily reserved for a garment of the finest quality, which was odd in itself since it was a cheap shirt, the sort one might buy in the men's section at Wal-Mart or Marshall's. It had a shine to it and the customer could see thin lines running through the fabric. It had been woven from polyester or nylon. The care devoted to the shirt seemed stranger still given that only the top of the shirt, the portion from the collar to the first button, could be seen. The rest was covered by the uniform of the establishment, a bright red smock that zipped up the front like a bowling shirt with the words "Papaya Queen" emblazoned on the back, and across the front, the motto of the store: "Snappy Service." The other employees wore t-shirts under their work coats, which seemed somehow more appropriate.

But nothing seemed quite so odd to the customer as how the man looked as he worked. The other men in the store went about their business haphazardly, frenzies of activity with no obvious direction or purpose. They had blank looks on their faces, or looks of despair or annoyance. It was apparent that they wanted to be anywhere but where they were. The blemished man was different. His work commanded the entirety of his concentration; his eyes suggested he was lost in thought. All the while he talked to himself, the orders muttered under his breath—"yes, yes, no"—obviously some kind of code known only to him. In some ways it seemed that he did not belong; in other ways it was difficult to imagine him being anywhere else.

"Two twenty-five."

When the order came up it took the customer by surprise. How could it be ready so quickly, he wondered? It seemed as if only a second or two had passed. Preparing hot dogs was not complicated work, but surely it took longer than this. Perhaps the movements of this unusual vendor had mesmerized him and he had lost track of time.

He reached into his pocket for money. He should have had it ready before. Now he felt pressure: the hot dogs were waiting, the people behind were waiting. He found three crumbled dollar bills in his front right pocket (there was no time to go to the wallet). He offered them to the man with some shame. The peculiar vendor made nothing of it. With a sweep of his hand he took the three dollar bills and replaced them with three quarters. The customer closed his fist around the change and shuffled the hot dogs off the counter, two into his free hand and, since he could not hold any more, one directly into his mouth.

He began to salivate immediately. He wanted to prolong the anticipation a bit, but he just could not wait and, presently, he allowed himself a bite. So good it was, crisp on the outside and moist on the inside, spiced just right, no other hot dog could compare. In an instant it was gone. He bit right into the second; it too promptly disappeared. He hesitated before getting into the third. His intention had been to bring one home for his wife as a surprise, but he could not resist the temptation. He constructed rationalizations. She would not be upset, he reasoned, since she would never know that he had even considered performing this favor for her in the first place. No one could be disappointed by a surprise not given. His conscience assuaged, the man bit in. The wave of flavor washed over him. Soon he forgot about his wife, and about the peculiar man who had served him his food. He was lost in the comfort of his frankfurter. Very few things in the world could make him feel better. He walked away from the store content.

Meanwhile, Mortimer went about his business.

"One with sauerkraut and mustard," a woman said.

Mortimer paused. The customer's voice had a raspy, sultry quality to it, and for a moment Mortimer wondered whether it might be she. But the voice was poutier, like a peeved teenage girl brooding over a too-early curfew. And he did not imagine that she would want sauerkraut and mustard. She would order it plain, to enjoy the full flavor of the frankfurter. She would not mask it in condiments, just as she did not mask her emotions in blather. No, this could not be her. Still, he looked up just to be sure.

It was not her, of course. This woman had some of the same features. She had dyed her hair platinum. She was thin and fit. She was pretty. But she was not *her*.

Mortimer's fingers flew through the work. One with sauerkraut and mustard, nothing to it. Quarter waiting at the finish.

"Two with sauerkraut."

"Four plain."

"One with mustard, one with mustard and sauerkraut."

The orders came rushing forward like a rising tide, which

Mortimer stemmed to the best of his ability. Some would have called his work dull. Some would have wondered how a man like Mortimer Taylor Coleridge, a man who had completed four semesters of coursework at Columbia University, could find fulfillment serving frankfurters at Papaya Queen. He would be the first to admit that there had been times when he would have asked these questions himself.

"Three with the works."

But he did not ask these questions anymore. He did not ask them because he no longer considered them relevant. Mortimer Taylor Coleridge was at peace with the world.

Mortimer Taylor Coleridge was in love.

3.

From the journal of Mortimer Taylor Coleridge

What is love?

Is it a force that can be harnessed, its energy channeled to propel man to soar to new heights, to achievements otherwise beyond his grasp? Or is it a raging scourge, a beast whose fury can never be contained?

Can we control it? Can we mold it to our purposes, turn it on and off like the lights in our kitchen? Or does it control us? Does it merely allow us to believe that we are in control as part of its master plan? Is it like the mother who offers her baby the pick of two bottles, each containing the same formula? Is the notion of control pure illusion?

Can it be mastered?

What is it? A thing? A path? A choice?

An emotion you say, but is this true? Can this conclusion be maintained upon considered reflection? We say that people are "in" love. This is not the way we speak of other emotions. We say that someone is sad, or that so and so is happy. Hubert is bilious. Francesca is dyspeptic. Is, is, is—always is.

When we say that someone is "in" something, we ordinarily speak of a place or a condition. He is in the hospital. Since her husband's death, she has been in a state of depression. Our use of language suggests a collective and sound intuition that love is more like a sickness than anything else. It surely has physical manifestations like an illness. It makes stomachs hurt and heads spin. It affects our ability to make rational decisions, so much so that we absolve people of responsibility for actions taken while under its influence. Forgive him for that, we will say, he is in love. Do we ever make allowances of this kind for someone who is happy or sad?

Love makes man want what he should never want, dream of what is not possible, desire those whom he should not desire. It emboldens him to try things he would never otherwise try. When he is finally out of its grasp, when he is sober, he shakes his head and wonders to himself, "did I really do that?"

What is it?

Can it be mastered?

In the No Doubt song "Bathwater" from the group's critically acclaimed fourth album, *Return of Saturn*, Gwen Stefani wonders about her attraction to a bad boy, someone who has had a "museum of lovers."

> *Wanted and adored by attractive women*
> *Bountiful selection at your discretion*
> *I know I'm diving into my own destruction*

Yet she plunges in anyway. She chooses the boy that is naughty, all the while aware that she is planting the seeds of her own destruction. Why?

> *No, I can't help myself*
> *I can't help myself*

Every day it happens, all over the world: people doing things they know not to be in their own interest, pursuing people they know are wrong for them, chasing follies, all in the name of love. They do it even as they know they are causing their own ruination. Why am I doing this, they ask. Why? Why?

But they cannot control themselves.

They are in love.

4.

"I said I love you."

Mortimer felt the shake on his arm, the shrill voice beckoning him back from his blissful meditations. He did not want to return. He was content in his dreams.

Another shake. Again the voice: "Are you listening to me? I said that I love you."

Why did she do it, he wondered? Why did she ask him a question that she knew he could not answer as she wanted, a question that by its very articulation would only add to her misery and to his. She had done it a thousand times before, each time with the same result: disappointment for her, discomfort for him. And yet she did it again, over and over. Why? Could she not help herself?

He turned and smiled.

"Thank you," he said.

Violet grimaced. She had a wisp of fine black hair on her upper lip. In the right light, it could not be seen, but when she curled her mouth downward the fur became conspicuous. It was not a flattering pose for her. Mortimer had told her this once, when she had been displeased with him about something or other, but it only had made a bad situation worse. "You don't think I'm pretty," she wailed. "Of course I do, of course I do," he said, patting her on the arm, anything to stop the sobbing. He learned his lesson after that, and never again mentioned this or any other aspect of her appearance. But this did not change the truth: he did not find the expression appealing.

He did not find any aspect of her appealing.

Violet Blayer was not pretty—this was safe to say—but her appearance was not distasteful either. She was tall for a woman, but not too tall to be awkward. She could have been thinner, but she could have been heavier too. When she wore a t-shirt or a baggy sweater she looked shapeless, an amorphous blob, but when she wore tighter clothes and the right sort of brassiere some curves appeared—not lip-smacking–come–hither curves, but curves all the same. In more desperate circles—prisons, last chance saloons—her body could have turned a head or two.

She had wiry, black hair, which she put up into a bun. The style did not flatter her. It better suited an old biddy than it did a thirty-three year old woman still bubbling with the ebbing percolations of hormone. But this was how Violet's mother wore her hair, so this was how Violet wore her own. Some of her features offset the harshness of the style. She had a gentle, expressive face, a mother's face. And her skin had resilience, the mixed curse and blessing of her Italian heritage. It had looked too old for her as a teenager, and it would look too good for her age when she grew into an old woman, but in the present, it seemed just right. The only blemish was a mole on her right cheek, coincidentally in almost precisely the same spot on her face as

Mortimer's stubborn ingrown hair was on his own. Some might say it marred her appearance. Others would say that it gave her character.

It all depended on the viewpoint of the observer.

So it was with the entirety of her appearance. She was an empty slate, a blank mat for those that looked upon her to impose their own conceptions of beauty. She could be comely or homely, fetching or repugnant; it all depended on the lens through which she was viewed. Violet Blayer was ordinary looking, in the same vague way the bulk of humanity might be described as ordinary looking, in the same meaningless way that one might have described Mortimer himself.

In a moment the grimace disappeared from her face.

"Tell me what you're writing about."

"You know I can't do that."

"You can," she said. "You choose not to."

Mortimer winced. He had corrected her in this fashion many times. He was a taskmaster when it came to good grammar, especially with her. Now she had used it against him. He would have to be more careful in the future. She was learning.

Mortimer realized that he would get no more done that evening. He closed the notebook and reached out from the bed to set it down on the night table. Then he laid the pen across its top, making sure to set it down perpendicular to the binding of the pad, or as close to it as one could achieve without the aid of a protractor. He lay back in bed.

"It's private," he said. "It's my personal journal. I've told you that before."

"I don't understand how it can be private. You write in it everywhere, at the museum, in the park. You start writing in it in the middle of conversations. If it were truly private you would only write in the privacy of your own home."

They had been through this a thousand times before.

"We've been through this a thousand times before," he said. "I told you that just because I write in public places doesn't mean that what I write is for public consumption. Sometimes I'm moved by things I hear or see, and I need to get the thoughts down as quickly as possible, otherwise they're lost forever. That doesn't mean that I sacrifice the right to keep those thoughts private. Perhaps someday I'll share them with the world. But when I choose, and on my own terms."

"It just doesn't seem healthy," said Violet. "It seems like you're missing out on things while they're happening. We're at the movies together and you're busy scrawling down quotes from the movie, impressions of the actors, whatever it is you do. But you don't actually see the movie. You can't record every experience. You need to live some of them . . . "

He began to drift again. Only isolated phrases made it through: "disengaged from life," "rude," and "the first time we went out." It was true what she said; he had begun writing on their first date, pizza and magazine shopping at the giant Barnes & Noble on 66th Street. Who remembered what she said that evening to set him off? But something had, and he pulled out his notebook and started writing in it right then and there. It hadn't bothered her. Nothing he did bothered her then. Things were easy, fresh and new. And she didn't just tolerate his writing, she embraced it. She said it made him seem deep and thoughtful. He liked that she liked it. He liked that she liked him.

Of course that was long before he found *her*. Now those early days of courtship seemed so long ago that he could not remember ever having had feelings for Violet. He had recorded them in his journal, so he believed they had existed, but they had long since faded. He had room in his heart for only one person. Even now, in the bedroom, his thoughts floated away to her, Violet's blather receding farther and farther into the background.

"My mother says you should give it up cold turkey . . ."

"I don't understand . . ."

Of course she didn't.

But *she* would.

5.

Papaya Queen is riddled with little signs that feature catchy slogans intended to move product. Each slogan is in quotes:

"Best Frankfurter in New York"
"Papaya is a Natural Digestive"
"Service With a Smile"

On more than one occasion Mortimer had attempted to explain to Bertrand Fuddle, the store manager, that the use of quotes indicated that the opposite of what the quotes contained was the truth.

"Thus," Mortimer said, "by writing 'Best Frankfurter in New York' in quotes instead of simply Best Frankfurter in New York, we suggest that our product is in fact not the best frankfurter in New York or, more damaging still, the worst frankfurter in New York."

It could not have been more plain, yet Bertrand Fuddle looked at Mortimer with disdain.

"This is better," he said.

"What do you mean?"

"This is better."

"I don't think you understand what I'm saying. The use of the quotes connotes precisely the opposite of the intended meaning . . ."

Bertrand Fuddle cut him off.

"Go sling the wieners."

Mortimer did not like the term wiener; it had a derogatory connotation, and he did not think of what he did as slinging. He considered himself to be an artist. Anyone who watched him could see this. Like a great ballerina, he performed with grace and efficiency of movement. He wasted no effort.

He did not like Bertrand Fuddle much either. Fuddle was a little rodent of a man with beady eyes, a blunted nose, and a fleshy face that wrinkled too much above the forehead when he kowtowed to one of his superiors or anyone else he regarded as important. He was a servile accounting type sent in by the mother corporation to make sure that the operation ran as efficiently as possible, and he cared not at all for the product. Mortimer had never seen Bertrand Fuddle take so much as a single bite of a Papaya Queen hot dog.

In the three years he had managed the Columbia University branch of Papaya Queen, Bertrand Fuddle had implemented a variety of profit-maximizing initiatives, almost all of which met with Mortimer's stern disapproval. For example, Fuddle began selling sausage, egg and cheese sandwiches during breakfast hours. Mortimer believed this fundamentally compromised the integrity of the institution. There should be a place in the world where one could go any time of day, 365 days a year, and buy a hot dog and nothing but a hot dog. For years Papaya Queen had been that place. Bertrand Fuddle put an end to that.

Mortimer protested. "Any place can make egg sandwiches," he said. "We do something special. We make the best hot dog in the world."

Bertrand Fuddle said, "This is better."

More controversially, Fuddle removed the tables from the front of the store. These three small booths were as old as the store itself and as integral to its history as the hot dogs. Students would sit at these booths for hours, reading the paper or doing a crossword or just watching the goings on. Some would spend the day studying for an exam, flaunting their ability to concentrate amidst such tremendous bustle, a geekish badge of honor. Computer science majors and artists alike coveted the places at the booths; they would wait them out for hours. Spending a day at a Papaya Queen booth was a landmark of the Columbia experience, as much as drinking on the roof of Butler Library, or having sex in its stacks.

Bertrand Fuddle took out the booths and replaced them with a thin counter. One night, at four a.m., without any warning so that no one would protest, he took out the tables and opened an entrance along 110th Street. This created a manageable flow of customers from the old entrance on Amsterdam Avenue to the new exit on 110th Street, where customers would now emerge by the B'nai Israel Synagogue next door. Opening the second entrance helped to bring order to Papaya Queen, but it displeased the membership of B'nai Israel—on Saturdays the lines for Shabbat services and for frankfurters would sometimes become confused—and displeased Mortimer for entirely secular reasons.

In the old days, chaos reigned at the ordering counter. People crammed in, squeezing through the old glass door, surging desperately towards the counter, as if rations of fresh water or life-saving drugs were being dispensed. No rules were imposed upon them. The store did not know from lines, just a mass of bodies pressing ever forward. The patrons did not mind the confusion. The coveted frankfurter became a holy grail, the effort to secure it a quest. They embraced the anarchy, as Mortimer himself had in his days as a student. It was part of what made him fall in love with the place.

The new manager dispensed of it with a snap of his fingers and the solemn pronouncement that "this was better." In doing so, he undermined Papaya Queen's essence. One doesn't tell people how to behave at a rock concert; he does not establish queues for people to join the mosh pit. The energy must be allowed to surge, lifting people where it will. This is part of the appeal of the rock show, to feel the loosed energy of thousands of humans packed tight into a single room, to feel alive, to feel the love.

Great people had the love.

Bertrand Fuddle did not have the love. He had the heart of an accountant. He ruined the place.

But this was all beside the point.

One of the signs with the quotation marks bothered Mortimer more than any of the others. It was prominently placed, just above the cash register at the Amsterdam Avenue side of the store, the point of ingress in Bertrand Fuddle's master plan. It hung alongside important signs such as:

"Papaya: Nature's Revitalizer"

"Recession Fighter: Filet Mignon on a Bun Still Only 75 Cents"

"We Love New York"

Go Bill Bradley Go!

America's "Great" Hot Dog Endorses America's Next "Great" President

(These were heady days for the Bradley campaign and Papaya Queen had thrown the full weight of its support behind the Senator.)

The sign in question said:

"Gutbuster: 3 Hot Dogs, Fries, Small Drink: $4.95"

It had been printed in red ink, with a casual font that made it look as if it had been written in crayon, though of course it had not been. Underneath this phrase, in extremely large type, were these words:

"What a Bargain!"

Underneath this, in fine print, had been added:

OJ, PJ not included.

These words were not enclosed in quotes.

The abbreviations "OJ" and "PJ" referred to orange juice and pineapple juice, two of the four kinds of beverages served at Papaya Queen. The disclaimer to the offer meant that someone ordering the Gutbuster could only select for their beverage papaya drink or a sweet coconut mixture called piña colada, which bore only a resemblance in color to the alcoholic refreshment of the same name.

The exclusion of orange juice and pineapple juice made some small difference to the store. Neither the piña colada drink nor the papaya drink contained any real juice. Both the OJ and PJ did have some real juice (though not one hundred percent as the name suggested) and juice cost money, even the frozen concentrated stuff that they threw into the beverage blenders at five in the morning when no one was looking. Thus the profit margin on orange juice and pineapple juice was merely ninety-seven percent, or something like that, as opposed to the papaya and piña colada drinks which, because they contained nothing even resembling juice, cost almost nothing. The store could make an entire batch of the papaya drink for less than fifty cents. This created approximately three hundred servings, which they sold for about ninety cents each, depending on whether the drink was ordered in connection with one of the specials. This in turn generated something on the order of a 54,000 percent rate of return on the initial investment in sugar, artifical flavoring, and unreinforced paper cups.

The papaya drink was noxious, vile stuff that tasted like poison. All of the regulars knew better than to order it. But a few times each hour, frequently enough to make the entire fifty-cent vat disappear by the end of the day, some unsuspecting rube would order a cup. They were out-of-towners usually, tourists who had heard of the famous Papaya Queen and figured a sample of papaya drink to be an integral part of the experience. It had to be good, they reasoned. After all, they had named the place for the stuff.

The moment of revelation that followed always played out in more or less the same way. The customer would inevitably let the drink sit in his mouth too long. They were all predisposed to liking the concoction, all the more so because they had already bitten into one of the hot dogs, which never ever disappointed. So they would wash it around in their mouth for a while, waiting for the wave of flavor that surely had to come. It never did. If anything the aftertaste was even worse, a bitter and coarse flavor that could not be explained by any of the individual ingredients. It was an evil brew, not of this Earth. The customer would spit it out then, almost always against the wall by the door on the 110th Street side of the store from which they had exited. A little stain had formed there, a faded patch in the pastel orange exterior of the store, worn white by the acidic projections of papaya. Some of the stain had spilled over onto the wall of the synagogue, further agitating the congregants of B'nai Israel.

But all of this was also beside the point.

What really bothered Mortimer Taylor Coleridge about the Gutbuster was its cost. Bought separately, hot dogs cost 75 cents each, $2.25 for three. An order of fries went for $1.25. A small glass of piña colada or papaya drink sold for 90 cents. Together the items totaled $4.40. Yet the Gutbuster sold for $4.95, fifty-five cents more than the items could be bought *a la carte*. Nothing else came with the Gutbuster—no fortune cookie or trinket, it did not come in a special box with a little hat. It was just the three hot dogs, fries, and the toxic beverage.

One day Mortimer went in to see Bertrand Fuddle to point out this anomaly. The manager had a small office in the back of the store. They had very little storage space, so the office had been filled with hot dogs buns and industrial-sized cans of ketchup and mustard. The only empty space was Fuddle's desk, which was strewn with paper, invoices and accounting receipts. On the front of his desk he had set a small plastic sign, the sort you might order through one of those advertisements inserted inside the comics section of the Sunday newspaper. It said:

B. Fuddle

"Manager"

"What is it?" asked Fuddle, not looking up from his paperwork.

"I wanted to talk to you about the Gutbuster," Mortimer said.

"What about it?"

"I think we should do away with it. It costs more than the individual items."

Fuddle looked up from his desk, peering at Mortimer over the rim of his reading glasses.

"This is better," he said and waved Mortimer out of his office.

6.

In the No Doubt song "Six Feet Under," Gwen Stefani asks the only question worth asking: What does it all mean?

> *Born to this life*
> *Where was I before?*
> *Non-existent? Not at all?*
> *Will I ever know?*

Professor Fillmore Skinny, chairman of the Columbia University biochemistry department and editor of the internationally esteemed journal *Post-Modern Genetics*, had an answer to this question: He believed that human beings were machines. For that matter, he believed that all living things were machines—intricate and diverse, unfathomable in their complexity, but machines all the same. And these elaborate mechanisms served the most unassuming of masters, a sticky porridge known to humans as nucleic acids.

Nucleic acids evolved on the planet Earth between four and five billion years ago. No one knows precisely how this happened. Some speculate that they may have arrived on an asteroid from another planet or galaxy. Others believe that they were placed here by mischievous folks from outer space, toying with the Earth as if it were some sixth-grade science project, like an Alka-Seltzer volcano. But even this explanation begs the question of how these impish budding scientists came to exist in the first place. The acids must have been created somewhere, sometime. Many scientists say it all happened in a giant bin of molten lava in the earliest days of the planet, in what scientists like to call the *primordial soup*.

"Campbell's Chicken Noodle," as Professor Skinny would say.

The nucleic acids were happy in the broth, but they were quite vulnerable. Any one of a host of menaces could undo them: a meteorite, an earthquake, an alien with a giant spoon. The nucleic acids were naked and could not move, so they were at nature's whim.

Over time some of them learned to build things, simple but useful things, things that we might think of as machines. They learned to build a protective membrane to shield themselves from the elements. They built machines with tiny fins that could swim across the soup to the warmer part of the pool where the nucleic acids liked it best. Later they built machines that could lift them up out of the soup so that they were no longer confined to the pool at all. The acids needed heat, so they built machines that could harness the energy of the sun. They even learned to make machines that could make copies of themselves.

Over the ages, they built more and more complicated machines, machines that could consume other machines, machines that could fly, machines that could scan other machines to see which one was the best. The best machines combined with one another to meld their programs and see if they might create a yet better machine.

The improved machines carried the nucleic acids wherever life might be sustained, to the sands of the desert, to the ice of the tundra, to the canopies of forests, which were composed of trees and ferns, machines themselves. Each territorial expansion improved the acids' fortune; each proliferation of a new type of machine gave them an added measure of security. The destruction of one would no longer mean the destruction of all.

Some of the more sophisticated machines gave the other machines names: ducks, emus, yellow-bellied sapsuckers. So varied they were in form and function that they suggested a multitude of purposes representative of their own diversity. But in truth the machines had only one purpose: to keep the nucleic acids alive. Their job was to reproduce and spread throughout the universe, to diversify the risk, so that the safety of the nucleic acids would be assured.

Some of these more sophisticated machines liked to believe otherwise. These machines fancied themselves to be in control. They believed they possessed free will, the ability to make choices. They pointed to the abundant evidence: People made choices every day, they said, choices such as what to wear, whom to sleep with, and whether to have green Jell-o or red.

Sometimes they made more difficult choices, moral choices, such as whether to tell the truth or to lie to someone to spare their feelings. They made complex choices about what to do with their money. They could choose, for example, to spend their money on sweet snacks, which they liked, or to give some of the money away to an organization that would use it to buy gruel and oranges, which would be fed to children who otherwise would have very little to eat. Some of the money given to these organizations would pay the salaries of directors, who would spend some of the money intended for the starving children on sweet snacks for themselves. This inefficiency, sometimes referred to as overhead, made the choice more complicated for the people choosing between donating the money and keeping it for sweets for themselves. But for better or worse the fact is they made a choice. The proof was in the pudding.

That these machines made choices proved nothing. They had been programmed to make choices. Their programming did not detail what they should do in every specific situation, such as whether they should spend money on dessert or give it to charity, but it specified general principles that could be applied to specific cases. Some of these principles included the notion that generosity is virtuous, corruption is bad, and that sex is better than almost anything else except sweet snacks. These maxims decided the machines' courses of action in specific cases.

"Poppycock!" said the machines that believed most fervently in their own sovereignty. If this were true then everyone would make the same choices. Everyone would give the money to charity, or not. Everyone would order the same flavor gelatin dessert. But they don't. People make different choices. Some people choose green Jell-o, others red. The fact that they made different decisions in identical situations proves that they are in control. It proves that they have free will.

The argument had some appeal to the smarter machines, but it proved nothing at all. The nucleic acids had simply created different programs for different machines. This protected them in the long run, in the same way it protected them to be carried to both the rain forest and the desert. If each machine made the same choice as all the other machines, the nucleic acids ran the risk that that choice could be the wrong one. Suppose, for example, that all of the big machines chose to live in Lubbock, Texas. This would be great for Lubbock and its economy, but what would happen if a giant boulder were to fall from the stars and flatten the entire city? All of the big machines would be destroyed and the nucleic acids would lose an important vehicle for carrying them around.

So they gave the machines different programs, different principles and preferences to guide them in their decisions. Some liked red better than green. Some gave everything to charity, some just a little bit, others nothing at all. Some liked it hot and chose to live in Lubbock. Some liked it cold and dark and lived in Minneapolis. Some would dissemble without hesitation; others would not think of lying, even if it meant saving their own life or, more importantly, the nucleic acids they carried.

Most liked sex a lot. This was important to the nucleic acids, as it kept them in contact with one another, allowing them to exchange information and diversify their programs. But even here the programs varied. Some of the machines could not go without sex for a day; others needed it less. Some didn't care for it much at all. Some liked boys, some liked girls, and some liked boys and girls.

The machines liked to believe that they were in control, but they were not. They had been programmed to think that they were in control, or at least to believe it was possible they might be in control. This made them do their job better. Some of the smarter machines would become less effective if they knew the truth. Their existence would seem pointless. Perhaps they would even rebel against their masters. In order to do their jobs well they needed to believe that they were in control. So the nucleic acids programmed them to believe this. It made them have more sex, which in turn made more nucleic acids.

This is how Professor Skinny would have answered Gwen's question: you were a glob of protein before you were born and will be again after you die. In the meanwhile your job is to have sex and move around a lot.

This is what Fillmore Skinny believed.

7.

In 1986, seventeen-year old John Spence approached his co-worker Eric Stefani with the idea of forming a band. Spence and Stefani worked at Dairy Queen, a chain of stores that got its start in 1938 in Kankakee, Illinois, where a man named Sherwood Noble sold delicious soft-serve ice cream for ten cents a cup. Noble's friends called him "Sherb."

Dairy Queen was an early pioneer of food franchising. In 1940, it opened its first outlet in Joliet, Illinois. Over the next ten years, they opened 2,000 more. Today, there are DQ franchises all over the world, including about 100 in Japan, where they used to sell hamburgers until the competition from McDonald's got to be too much and they switched to pitas.

Spence and Stefani worked at the Dairy Queen in their hometown of Anaheim, California. Stefani liked Spence's idea about forming a band. He signed on and recruited his sister Gwen, then a high school senior, to sing backing vocals.

Spence and the Stefanis and the sixteen-year old bass player Tony Kanal were all taken with a type of Jamaican dance music known as *ska*. Ska is instrumented with lots of brass and a Hammond organ, like the one played at baseball games, and is characterized by a pronounced and distinctive syncopation.

The drum comes in on the downbeats of the second and fourth beats of each measure; the guitar rests upon the first beat and then emphasizes the remaining upbeats. It sounds a little like someone with the hiccups singing from inside the bell of a tuba. The name comes from one of the early practitioners of the art, the bassist Cluet Johnson, who liked to greet people with the phrase "Love Skavoovie," which as far as anyone can tell doesn't mean much of anything at all.

Ska was as much a social movement as it was a musical genre. Radio wasn't popular in Jamaica in the 1950s. Instead, enterprising businessmen brought music to the masses through giant sound systems, which traveled around the island blasting new music. They played ska on these traveling boom boxes, and the people loved it, especially the legion of disaffected, unemployed Jamaicans living in the ghettos of Kingston. Though jobless, these *rude bwoys* dressed in the best fashion of the day: narrow-brim hats, dark suits, and thin ties. They also made lots of noise and fought in the streets and generally caused a commotion.

Some of the early ska songs told their story. Desmond Dekker, the first ska musician to reach the charts, sang about them:

> *Them a loot, them a shoot,*
> *Then a wail, at Shanty Town*
> *When rude boy deh 'pon probation*
> *Then rude boy a bomb up the town.*

Desmond Dekker's song was a bit of a downer, but most of the music had a more optimistic outlook, and it could be danced to, and best of all, it belonged to the people. The Jamaicans embraced the music. Cecil Bustamente Campbell, later known as Prince Buster expressed the motto of the ska movement. He said: "Enjoy yourself. It's later than you think."

Then, just as it got really popular in the summer of 1967, ska disappeared. It can get to be hot as heck in Jamaica. It did that summer and the idea of dancing in the sticky sooty streets seemed less appealing to the people. This is the way it is sometimes with young people—they get worked up into a lather about one thing or another and then it gets really hot outside and they head for the beach and forget about what it was that ever excited them in the first place. Young people do not have staying power. Jamaican musicians slowed down their tunes and ska morphed into something called rocksteady and then into reggae, which is precisely the right sort of music to encourage someone to sit on the beach and do nothing.

Then, no sooner than it had left, ska came back. This is also how it is with young people. Sometimes they absolutely have to have the thing that they threw in the garbage the day before. Young people are impetuous. This goes hand in hand with the absence of staying power.

This new version of ska was less threatening than the original. The rude boys lost the "w" in their name, which many people had found as threatening as their menacing attitude, which they also dropped. They wore two-tone suits now and pork-pie hats and seemed most interested in having a good time. This music spread. Bands with names like the Specials and Madness became popular in England and then the United States.

One of Madness's most famous songs is about a young man on his sixteenth birthday who claims the privileges of majority: It is called "Welcome to the House of Fun."

John Spence and the Stefanis liked Madness very much and decided to play ska themselves. They called their band "No Doubt" after an expression that John liked to use. People in California use the words in the way that people on the East Coast use the phrase "I see" or "okay." For example, one could imagine this exchange occurring on the streets of Anaheim:

> Hubert: "The new humidifier I bought is doing a fine job."
> Ignatius: "No doubt."

> Sometimes the phrase is used for emphasis, as in:
> Stan: "Brenda has a winning smile."
> Mordecai: "No doubt."

> On occasion it can create confusion, as with:
> Grady:"The No Doubt show promises to be extraordinary."
> Parson Willis: "No doubt!"

But this is the way people talk in California, and Mortimer Taylor Coleridge liked to imagine that John Spence embraced the potential confusion that might have arisen from the name. It seemed to be the sort of thing he would have liked. He was an effervescent boy who danced and did back flips and commanded the stage. No Doubt was his band in those early days. They played at house parties and clubs in Southern California, singing songs like "Big City Train," which went:

This time I'll board that train; it won't be long
Check the label on my baggage; destination in my song
Talk to the conductor; saved up my fare
Yakety-yak for a while
CHOO CHOO!

Gwen just sang backup then, a gangly and awkward presence on the stage, trying to stay out of the way of John's stage antics. By all accounts she offered little hint of the star she would become. The band didn't seem to know exactly what she was doing there. Neither did she. Soon she would, though. Just before Christmas in 1987, one week before the band was supposed to perform in front of a room of record industry executives, John Spence drove to a neighborhood park in Anaheim and shot himself in the head.

He left a suicide note explaining how his few possessions should be dispersed and why he was doing what he was doing. It said: "I think I've felt too much pain and all I see in my future is more." After John's death, the band considered breaking up then decided that he would have wanted them to stay together. Gwen became the lead singer.

Sometimes life works this way.

Welcome to the House of Fun.

In the days after seeing the *Behind the Music* profile, Mortimer Taylor Coleridge learned everything there was to learn about Gwen Stefani and her band. Violet facilitated the process by buying Mortimer compact discs from the store where she worked as a clerk, Skyscraper Records. Skyscraper Records called itself this even though nobody in the United States had bought a new record album in ten years. Now everyone buys 1.2 millimeter-thick discs of polycarbonate plastic, which are silk-screened with a spiral track of pits, each 100 nanometers deep by 500 nanometers wide, that function as a form of binary data. Describing this, however, would have made a less romantic name for a store.

Skyscraper gave its workers a "15% Employee Discount—Sale Items Excluded." This was still a good deal for the store since it marked the merchandise up by approximately 600%. A compact disc costs about seventy cents to make, including the few pennies paid to the band for its sweat and heartache. Manufacturers sold the discs to distributors like Skyscraper Records for two dollars. In turn Skyscraper sold it for fourteen dollars or so. This was not quite as good a return as Papaya Queen made on papaya juice, but it was pretty good all the same, even with the fifteen percent employee discount—sale items excluded.

Violet bought Mortimer copies of all four No Doubt CDs: the self-titled debut album, which sold poorly, the *Beacon Street Collection*, a compilation of songs written at the depths of the band's despair, their breakthrough *Tragic Kingdom*, and the triumphant *Return of Saturn*. Violet asked no questions; she was pleased Mortimer had taken an interest in something, pleased that she could please him.

Mortimer listened to the new CDs over and over, for weeks on end, studying the lyrics as if they were poetry, looking for the insight they might offer him into Gwen's soul. He searched the Internet to learn what he could about her. He read biographies of the band and interviews with the individual members. He even read through fan web sites, mindless prattle filled with pilfered pictures of the band and ruminations by this person or that about why they loved Gwen, as if they ever could. Though these sites had nothing of interest for him, he read them anyway, methodically working his way through them all on the chance, however slight, that he might find something meaningful, some bit of knowledge that might allow him to better understand her.

Then one day, at gwenforever.com, a profile of the singer with her birthday and education and scattered facts that any amateur could have put together, Mortimer found something new:

Favorite Food: Papaya Queen Hot Dogs

This is how it all began.

8.

From the journal of Mortimer Taylor Coleridge

This news about Gwen excites and pleases, but does not surprise. The popularity of the frankfurter knows no bounds. Americans alone consume about two billion pounds of hot dogs each year, about twenty billion hot dogs, which amounts to sixty hot dogs for every man, woman, and child in the country. More than one in four call it their favorite food.

This broad appeal is no recent phenomenon. The consumption of sausage can be traced back to the Babylonians, as early as 1500 B.C. It is mentioned in the writings of Homer. Historians believe it to have played an important role in the Roman festival of Lupercalia—some accounts suggest that the links may have played a role beyond mere food—before the Roman Catholic Church declared sausage eating a sin and the Emperor Constantine banned its consumption.

The origin of the modern version of the food is a subject of some dispute. According to some accounts, in the early 1850s the Frankfurt butchers guild introduced a spiced, smoked sausage packed in a thin casing. They named it a "frankfurter" after their hometown and claimed it as their own. Around the same time a similar sausage appeared in Vienna. No one can say which came first.

Like their German counterparts, the Viennese butchers named the sausage for their hometown, a "wiener." In both cities the new sausage had a slightly curved shape due to, according to the German version of the story, the influence of a young Frankfurt butcher who had a special fondness for his dachshund. The food thus also came to be known as a "dachshund sausage," the name that it carried to America.

Precisely when it arrived in the United States is again a matter of some dispute. Reports exist of German immigrants selling dachshund sausages, along with milk rolls and sauerkraut, in the Bowery as early as the 1860s. Charles Feltman, a German butcher, opened the first Coney Island frankfurter stand in 1871. He sold 3,684 dachshund sausages in his first year of business.

The food skyrocketed in popularity in the 1890s when Chris Ahe, the owner of the St. Louis Browns baseball team, began to sell frankfurters at the ballpark. In 1901, on a cold April day, vendors hawked frankfurters from portable hot water tanks shouting, "They're red hot! Get your dachshund sausages while they're hot!" The story goes that Tad Dorgan, a sports cartoonist observing the scene, drew a hasty sketch of barking dachshund sausages nestled in warm rolls. Not sure how to spell "dachshund," he wrote simply "hot dog." But no one has ever unearthed this cartoon, despite Dorgan's popularity. Others believe that Yalies may have coined the term in the 1890s when they referred to frankfurter carts as "dog wagons," a skeptical judgment on the origin of the food.

Questions about the composition of frankfurters trace back

as far as the food itself. A popular song of 1860, which has been modified over the decades, went:

Oh where oh where has my little dog gone?
Oh where oh where can he be?
Now sausage is good, baloney, of course.
Oh where oh where can he be?
They make them of dog, they make them of horse,
I think they made them of he.

In fact most hot dogs generally contain meat taken from the muscle of the animal, combined with spices such as garlic, salt, corriander, and pepper. The key ingredients in Papaya Queen hot dogs are sugar, which makes the frankfurter sweet and moist, and ground mustard, which gives it tang and kick. This information is kept secret from the masses to help preserve the frankfurter's mystique.

The question presents itself then: why is the hot dog so popular? Why, if people suspect it to contain all kinds of unspeakable things they would never otherwise consider eating, do they continue to devour the food with such relish?

The popularity of hot dog substitutes offers some insight to the answer. Papaya Queen hot dogs contain one hundred percent beef. Granted it is not from the same cut as a good steak, but everything in it comes from a cow. Beef hot dogs are far and away the most popular type of frankfurter, but alternatives abound, such as low fat hot dogs, chicken hot dogs, turkey hot dogs. Even vegetarians have a host of options including hot dogs made from soy, tempeh and other meat substitutes. The prevalence of these hot dog surrogates suggests that the popularity of the hot dog stems from something other than its composition and taste. It suggests that it derives from something much more basic, something that is so elementary that most fail even to notice it and at the same time so powerful that it helps to explain the very nature of man's existence. The essence of its appeal rests in its shape.

To appreciate this, one must first accept the self-evident axiom that the line is the fundamental form of life. When the nucleic acids advanced their way out of the primordial soup, they did so by learning to harvest energy. They built machines capable of taking in energy in all of its various forms, from the simplest, like sunlight, to the most complex, like chocolate milk and moose dung, absorbing what could be used and discarding the rest. The machines used the extracted energy to do things that helped ensure the survival of the nucleic acids, such as moving from place to place, having sex, and assembling patio furniture.

The sacred path through which energy is taken in and given off is a straight line. Take as an example the worm, the most basic of macro-organisms. Energy enters the worm through its mouth in whatever form the slithering creature happens to find it. Any type of organic matter will do; decomposed human tissue is a particular favorite. The food is then passed through the digestive tract of the worm by a process called peristalsis, an alternation of contraction and expansion that squeezes food through the system. Along the way, the crawler absorbs whatever it can put to use. The rest is discarded through its anus.

The worm is an eating machine. It eats and drinks constantly (worms produce sixty percent of their body weight in urine every day), pausing only for sex, which they especially like to have in the rain when they can flop about on the surface without fear of dehydration. It is easier to find a mate on flat, open ground than in their subterranean tunnel homes.

Sex is a peculiar act for the worms. They are hermaphroditic; any worm can form a union with any other worm. They mate by lying head to tail with their friend, producing a temporary skin canal through which sperm flows from one worm into the other. The girdle-like ring around the front of the worm, called the clitellum, then slides down the body, picking up egg and sperm along the way. The tube then falls off the worm forming a nest for the newly fertilized eggs.

When these eggs hatch, baby worms begin their own lives of burrowing through soil or animal intestine or wherever they make their home, eating their way through the days, until they are ready themselves to renew the process by having sex and making more eating machines.

And so on.

Because of the structure of the worm and the shape of its digestive tract, the process is facilitated by the ready availability of moist food in a cylindrical form that can easily slide its way through the worm intestine. Say, for example, a tiny hot dog.

People fancy the world to be filled with a rich mosaic of animal life, and it is in some sense, but the differences are not nearly so extensive as the commonalities. The similarities are easiest to see in some animals, like crocodiles and snakes, which seem like nothing more than big worms—slightly larger eating machines that feast on more substantial prey than leaves and dead skin. But the congruencies do not end with these creatures. Take, for example, the bird. Upon examination, the bird is revealed to be nothing more than a modified worm, a linear eating machine with a beak to peck at seeds and sap and other tasty treats and wings and webbed feet to carry it from one place to another. In fact the behavior of the bird is little different from that of the worms: it spends most of its days eating and flitting about, with occasional interruptions for sex, though it has no predilection for rain or any other weather.

So it is true of every animal. Giraffes are worms with long necks and tall legs for reaching food in tall trees. They spend most of their days moving about and eating, with occasional interruptions for sex. Turtles are worms with thick shells to protect them from predators and webbed feet to propel them through water. They spend most of their days moving about slowly and eating, with occasional interruptions for sex. Humans are worms with big brains, which are useful for constructing elaborate defenses from predators, such as bullet proof vests and orbital missile shields, and opposable thumbs, which help open hard-to-reach foods like macadamia nuts and tins of smoked sardines. Humans spend most of their days moving about and eating, with occasional interruptions for sex.

At its core, the human being is nothing more than a tall

worm. A worm with arms and legs and ear hair and mouth rot, but a worm all the same. Indeed, the human digestive system looks very much like a worm. It is called the alimentary canal. Food passes through the alimentary canal in the same manner it passes through the digestive tract of the worm, by a series of alternating contractions and expansions that squeezes food through the system. The body absorbs what it can use; the rest is excreted through the anus.

Because of the structure of the alimentary canal, the process of digestion is facilitated by the consumption of moist food in cylindrical form that can easily slide its way through the intestinal tract.

Say, for example, a hot dog.

9.

Late one summer night, Mortimer found himself alone inside the Papaya Queen. This almost never happened. Even at the oddest of hours, stragglers would wander into the store: hungry drunkards on their way home from the bars, an expectant mother with a frankfurter craving, an early riser with no good breakfast options. But the city had been emptied out that evening, the middle night of a holiday weekend.

Mortimer had volunteered to work the night shift. This enabled some of the other employees to take vacations with their families. Mortimer did not have much family and had little desire to visit what remained of it. In any event, he did not believe in the value of vacations. The schedule also gave him an easy excuse to avoid seeing Violet, who had mentioned a plan to go down to the Jersey Shore and see fireworks, or something dreadful like that.

Violet protested at first. "You love working more than you love me," she bawled. This was true, of course, though work was not the only thing he loved better than her. But Mortimer lied and said it was not the case, that there had been no one else available for the shift. He said he would make it up to her in some other way, which he had no intention of doing, but saying so placated her and finally she went off to her mother's for the weekend, mercifully leaving him in peace.

Mortimer loved having the store to himself. He loved being able to hear the sounds that the cacophonous frenzy of activity drowned out during the day: the soft whirring of the juice spinners, the popping of the oil in the Fry-o-lator, the hum of the fluorescent lights.

He also loved the aroma of the frankfurters. In the daytime, the putrid odor of humanity masked the scents; now he smelled pure, unadulterated beef product, wafting through the air, tickling his nose.

Best of all he loved being in control. Since Bertrand Fuddle had gone home for the weekend, the store was his and his alone.

It was a perfect night, the sort of evening New York enjoys only once or twice a summer, cool and crisp, without any of the usual stickiness. What few people had remained over the weekend moved slowly. The city lacked the critical mass of people to invest the stragglers with the accustomed sense of urban urgency. People ambled along the sidewalks. Cars waited patiently at the traffic light at the corner of 110th and Amsterdam. No one honked. The city was at peace.

Mortimer absently whistled to himself, "Don't speak, I know just what you're saying." He craned his neck to look up at the sky; he could see a star or two, the air was that clear. He watched it all contentedly.

Mortimer Taylor Coleridge was in love.

Around half past three in the morning, a man entered the

store, a fat man with a mop of gray hair and a scraggy beard and a belly that hung over his jeans. He looked a little like the notorious pornographer Al Goldstein, but Mortimer couldn't be sure if it was he. This man, whoever he was—pornographer or not—wore a black t-shirt, one size too small. It said:

Why Ask Why?

This had once been the slogan of a popular beer. The advertising campaign had been designed to generate good will for the beer by mocking situations in which people ask difficult, sometimes unanswerable questions. The campaign more subtly aimed to discourage people from asking thoughtful questions at all, questions such as why they chose the beer they chose. Suppressing such inquiries had special importance to the corporate behemoth that owned the beer, since its product was no better than that of many of its competitors, yet it charged more than twice as much for its beer as other companies did.

Ordinarily it would not be possible to say that one beer was better than another or not since taste is subjective, but in this case the advertising executives could be quite sure of the similarity. The company that owned the popular beer also owned one of its main competitors, a discount label called U-Sav-A-Lot. U-Sav-A-Lot beer and the popular beer were both brewed at the same distillery in St. Louis, Missouri. In fact they were the same beer. The only difference was the bottles into which the beer was poured, how the beers were advertised, and what people were willing to pay. People paid extra for the popular beer because they associated it with girls in bikinis and witty talking lizards. Of course the people who bought the popular beer did not believe that they liked it for this reason. They believed the popular beer tasted better than the others did. This is an example of what marketing executives call subliminal advertising. People believe they are buying something because it is better when in fact they are buying it because they have pictures of girls in bikinis flashing in their minds.

This was good news for the advertising people and especially for the beer makers. They made a lot of money on U-Sav-A-Lot beer. A gallon of beer costs only about fifty cents to make. This generated a profit margin of about eighty percent. They made even more on the popular beer. For this brand they had a profit margin of about four hundred percent. This was not as good as the profit margin on Papaya Drink, but it was still pretty good, and a heck of a lot better than eighty percent.

Beer companies did lots of advertising.

Relatively speaking, "Why Ask Why?" had not been a successful advertising campaign. In fact it had been a complete bust. It did not feature any pretty girls or funny animals or any of the usual things that moved product. It confused people; they didn't understand the commercials, and this made them angry. After a few months, the corporation abandoned the campaign. Its executives fired the agency that had developed the ad. The old agency said it was *cutting edge*. Now the corporation used a more traditional advertising firm, which only made commercials with talking animals and girls in bikinis.

The corporation liked to pretend that the old advertising

campaign had never happened. In this endeavor they had been quite successful. Most people could not remember the slogan unless reminded of it, and even then many still could not remember the product with which it had been associated. But this man did. As part of its efforts to promote the slogan, the beer company gave t-shirts with the slogan away at a funny car show in Teaneck, New Jersey. The customer got one. He liked funny cars. He liked t-shirts too, especially free ones. He wore his with great pride, so much pride that it was, in fact, his favorite t- shirt.

Mortimer hated it. On another day he might have hated the man for wearing it. But Mortimer had no room for hatred in his heart on that cool summer's night, only love. He gave the man a smile.

The man in the t-shirt took his time ordering, too long really. They had only hot dogs and French fries and drinks on the menu. But the customer felt the need to read through every sign in the store. On a busier day Mortimer would have hurried him along, but not that night. That night he had all the time in the world.

Finally the customer was ready.

"I'll have two Gutbusters," he said. "With the works."

Instinctively, Mortimer's fingers reached for the hot dogs and the condiments. Then he stopped himself. He felt uncharacteristically charitable.

"You know," Mortimer said, looking up from the hot dog grill, "it would be cheaper for you if you bought everything separately."

This caught the man in the t-shirt by surprise. He took the smallest of steps backwards, as if Mortimer's act of speaking to him had been an effrontery.

"Excuse me?"

"I said it would be cheaper for you if you bought everything separately."

This time the man thought for a moment about Mortimer's words.

"I don't understand," he said.

"Look," Mortimer explained. "Two Gutbusters cost $9.90. Individually, six hot dogs cost $4.50. Two orders of fries is another $2.50. And two drinks run you $1.80. All together that's $8.80, a dollar and ten cents less than the Gutbusters. And if you buy a large drink instead of the two small drinks, you could save another forty cents and get more to drink."

Confusion washed over the customer's face; the math had dizzied him. He turned it over and over in his mind, looking for the error that he knew the reasoning must contain. He did not trust Mortimer. The customer stared at Mortimer accusatorily, as if Mortimer stood somehow to profit from this scheme he had proposed.

"I think I'll stick with the Gutbuster," the man said derisively. He pointed to the sign above Mortimer's head. "It's a bargain," he said. "I prefer the bargain."

This recalled to Mortimer the Robert Frost poem about the two neighbors who meet every year to mend the wall between their property. The wall serves no purpose. They have nothing to fence in or fence out, nor any disputes between them. Yet they mend the wall every year. When the narrator questions the neighbor as to why they do it, the neighbor mindlessly chants a mantra his father had once taught him, as his father's father had before that: "Good fences make good neighbors." The fence mender does not know the logic behind the slogan; he does not care to. He just fixes the fence.

After that the narrator watches his neighbor repair the wall: "He moves in darkness as it seems to me." The man in the t-shirt seemed to move in darkness now, obediently repeating to himself his own mantra: "What a Bargain! What a Bargain!" He did not consider the logic behind it; he did not care to.

Why Ask Why?

Mortimer's better judgment told him to leave it at that, but he could not restrain himself. The man's order was an offense against reason, and he had an obligation to lead him out of the darkness.

"Look, friend," Mortimer said, "you're making a mistake. It doesn't make any difference to me. I'm just trying to help you."

The man in the t-shirt straightened his neck.

"You think I'm making a mistake?"

"I do. You could save over a dollar and get more to drink."

"You think you know better than me."

Mortimer saw the signals that he had raised the man's ire. He spoke with more caution now.

"In this particular case I do."

"If you're so smart," the customer said smugly, "how come

you work in a hot dog store?"

Mortimer started to say that he had gone to Columbia University, that he had been an evolutionary biology major and a budding geneticist, that he had studied under Professor Fillmore Skinny, one of the greatest minds of the twentieth century. He started to say that he knew multivariable calculus and that he could multiply two three-digit numbers in his head. He started to say that his mind could dance rings around the pathetic man in the dated t-shirt. But he caught himself. The man would not believe any of it, and it would mean nothing to him even if he did believe it. So Mortimer said nothing.

The man in the t-shirt snorted out his nose and shook his head. "You should be ashamed of yourself. How many people a day do you get to go for that trick? All so that you can pocket a few extra bucks."

"I should tell your boss," he went on. "I should tell your boss, but I won't. I won't because I feel sorry for you. You probably need that money to feed some bastard kid of yours or for some liquor or a drug fix. So I'm gonna cut you a break."

The man's pants had slipped down, and his stomach peeked out from beneath the too-small t-shirt.

"Now let me have my bargain. Let me have my Gutbusters."

Mortimer remembered something his grandmother had once said to him: "the heart wants what it wants." She did not say it apropos of anything. She just said things like this from time to time because she liked the way they sounded.

Good fences make good neighbors.

Why Ask Why?

Mortimer's fingers danced across the grill. Six hot dogs with sauerkraut and sauerkraut. Two orders of fries. Two small papaya drinks. He cupped a dime in his palm, anticipating the change that would be due.

Mortimer handed the food and drink over to the man.

"Anything you say," he said. "Come again soon."

10.

From the journal of Mortimer Taylor Coleridge

I have just had the dream again.

In the dream I am waking from a dream. She is in my arms, still asleep, her head resting in the small between my shoulder and chest. She is warm, warm as a child. I watch her stomach rise and fall, a gentle soothing motion. She has curves. Her skin is soft and wet. I am happy.

She stirs, and at first is disoriented. Her eyes search about the still unfamiliar apartment. It does not displease her, but this is not what they are seeking. They are searching for me. Soon enough they find me. Contentment washes over her face as she looks into my eyes. I have never looked better than I look in the reflection of her lens. She is quiet, does not want words, does not need words to say what she means. I know that I am loved and understood, as she is. We are happy.

The dream comes more and more often now. It feels so true.

It is sometimes hard to say what is the dream.

And what is reality.

I wonder why I love her so. It would be easy to say that it is nothing more than a crush, that she is of no more real significance than the pin-up girl in the calendar. After all, I do not know her. I know only the face she shows on television and magazine covers and that is not the real person. So it cannot be true love. It would be easy to say this, I know, but it is not true.

There have been crushes before: Stacey Capasso in the third grade, Mrs. Periwinkle the home economics teacher, the counter girl at the Roy Rogers. Some celebrities too: Farrah Fawcett, Christie Brinkley. The picture of Stevie Nicks on the cover of *Rumors* haunted me during my teenage years. I told myself I was in love on all of these occasions too. But I did not know what the word meant then. The feelings I have now have nothing in common with those. This is so much more.

She is truly beautiful. Her body is toned, lithe and sinewy, her face bright and expressive. She is in perfect balance. She has luxuriant, flowing hair, but not too much. She is curved but not too curved, her stomach tight like a swimmer's. She is feminine, but not overly feminine. When she dances she seems sometimes to slip out of her gender. It does not diminish her appeal; it is the essence of it.

No doubt this is part of it. No doubt.

Fancies for pretty girls ebb over time. They cannot be sustained. When they are summoned back years later, in some moment of need, the mental snapshot of the person can be recalled, but not the feelings. It is a struggle to remember whether there ever were feelings at all. This is because these pashes are empty at their core. They are lustful flashes, hormonal surges, gone in a moment.

This is different. This is growing, evolving.

It is different because it is her mind that I love. Some people in the world ask no questions. They live in blissful ignorance, content to move in darkness. They do not desire to know what their place in the world is, whether any of it means anything more. It is easier this way. The truth would overwhelm them. Better for them to keep their eyes shut.

Other souls are more restless. These souls search to find their way. They ask every question. They want to know it all, no matter what the truth may be. These are the people worth knowing. These are the people who can be loved. The others can be desired, lusted after, objectified. But the potential object of true, transcendent love must be one who wants more. This person must desire consciousness. He or she must join in the search for meaning. These souls are few. Hers is surely one of them. I hear it in the music. I hear her asking aloud the questions that we all ask ourselves. Who am I? Do I control my own fate? Is this all there is?

The radio pours out babble, mindless jabber that soothes the masses. It deadens their minds, clucking gently to them as they sink into lower and lower states of being, nodding their heads to the rhythms all the while. Through this prattle, her voice cuts like a laser, a Picasso on a wall of kindergarten finger paintings, a Chateau d' Rothschild in a rack of vinegar, poetry in a sea of drivel.

The makeup's all off
Who am I?
If the magic's in the make up
Then who am I?

She is calling out, searching for someone, searching for someone asking these same questions.

She is calling out to me.

Movie actors, billionaires, pop stars—she can have anyone she desires. But these men have nothing for her. They live in the world of luxury, their every need and whim catered to: big cars to drive in, women to affirm their virility, sycophants to stroke their ego. They do not ask the hard questions. It is not convenient for them. They are too comfortable.

She will dabble with them. She must. She is a searching soul, so she must sample it all. But she can find no lasting comfort in any of it. In time she will wonder if there is more. The men, misunderstanding her restlessness, will offer her larger homes and bigger diamonds. But she does not want for things. She yearns for awareness and they cannot help her in this.

But I can. I can help her in her journey. I can help her to be happy.

I understand. I understand her.

She will find me, I know that. You will not read of any stalking in these pages, no mad obsessions. That is not where any of this is going. Just as people cannot change who they are, so too are preordained many of the paths they must travel down. Saying this does not suggest a belief in fate or any god on my part. It has nothing to do with any of that silliness. It is only a logical extension of an enlightened understanding of the nature of man, and the nature of life. If man's appearance is programmed at birth, if his personality is imprinted, the criteria he will use to make his choices are formed before he is even aware of his own existence. If he is no more than a machine, then the path that he will follow has been determined before he is even born. Knowing this path is just a matter of understanding well enough how each individual machine has been built.

She will come. She must. The only question is when.

I do not worry about any of this. The question that plagues me is quite different. It keeps me up through the night, staring at the ceiling. I do not know how to begin to approach it. The question is this: how am I to prepare? How am I to make sure that when the moment comes the optimal outcome will be achieved, the outcome that will save both her and me? Because while I have the quiet confidence that she has no choice but to cross my path, I have great doubt that she will recognize me for what I am—the man most in need of her, and he with the most to offer her. And I doubt too that she shall ever pass my way again.

It has been months now since I first discovered her and I am no closer today to understanding the road I am supposed to follow to her. Life is rolling by, but I am adrift, a man with a destination and a direction but no boat to steer or arms to swim.

So this is what I worry about. What will be required of me when the moment comes? How am I to make myself ready for the encounter?

It is the simplest question of all: What should I do?

11.

Papaya Queen stays open 24 hours a day, 365 days a year, which creates staffing problems during holidays. That year, Mortimer volunteered to work a shift on Christmas Eve. He did it partially in the hope that Violet would again decide to spend the holiday with her mother, and partially because he coveted quiet time in the store so much.

Violent became upset when she found out, demanding to know why he so often offered to work on the holidays. He explained to her that others had families and religious convictions, and had more need of the time as a result. And besides, they would spend Christmas Day together. The compromise satisfied Violet, who wanted to spend Christmas Eve with her mother anyway. In the afternoon she kissed him goodbye and said she would see him in the morning. She seemed happy.

It turned out to be a wonderful night at the store, almost magical. Despite the holiday, people drifted in—the hardcore regulars who could not go without their fix, scattered atheists grateful to find anything open at that time on a holiday evening—an eclectic group, more appreciative than ever for the perpetual availability of the product. Mortimer felt important and needed; it reminded him why he had gotten into the business in the first place.

At around 11:30, about halfway into Mortimer's shift, Bertrand Fuddle came in. He wore a green polyester blazer and a bright but tattered Christmas tie, a shabby effort at dressing for the holiday. He blended in well with the store, which itself had been half-heartedly decorated for the season. Tinsel dangled haphazardly from the ceiling. Above the beverage area along the back wall had been hung a silver and blue banner. It said:

"Merry Christmas"

The "C" in Christmas, which sagged at the lowest point of the sign, hung directly over another sign, which said:

Orange Juice

Loaded With Vitamin "C"

Fuddle had graciously volunteered to work that evening, thereby freeing the holiday for one of his employees. The staff appreciated the gesture. But when Mortimer saw Fuddle come in early for his shift he wondered whether the manager might have arranged the schedule so that he could check up on Mortimer. If this were true, it would have angered Mortimer. Even the prospect of it upset him. But it did not seem to be the case. Fuddle just sort of hung around the store, puttering about in his office for a bit, then wandering out into the sales area where he made some idle chitchat with Mortimer between customers. In three years, Bertrand Fuddle had never before made idle chitchat with Mortimer.

"What are your plans for the holiday?" Fuddle asked.

"Nothing special."

"Will you be spending it with Violet?"

It surprised Mortimer to hear that Fuddle knew of his relationship. Violet had been to the store a few times before. She occasionally met Mortimer after work since Skyscraper Records was only a few blocks away. Once she had come by to bring him something that he had forgotten. But Mortimer had not realized that Fuddle noticed any of this. He was particularly surprised that Fuddle knew Violet's name.

"I suppose," Mortimer said.

"She seems like a sweet girl."

Mortimer nodded.

"Did you get her something nice?"

"I didn't buy her anything," said Mortimer. "I don't celebrate Christmas."

"She does though, yes?"

"She does, but she understands that I do not feel the need to celebrate the holiday with the exchange of material items. It's such an artificial sentiment."

Fuddle smiled weakly. "I suppose," he said. Then he stepped back. A customer was waiting.

A man in a Santa Claus suit ordered three with the works. The outfit did not fit him well. He wore a plaid flannel shirt, which had not been tucked into his pants, and could be seen under the traditional red suit. His white beard and hair had been glued on with little care, leaving his own natural beard visible, as well as his frizzy black hair. He paid for the hot dogs in change, nickels and dimes mostly. A bottle of Miller High Life hung out of his coat pocket.

Seeing Saint Nick, it occurred to Mortimer then to ask Fuddle about his own holiday. Mortimer knew almost nothing about Fuddle since before that night they had never had a personal conversation. Mortimer envisioned Fuddle in the suburbs, with a wife who spent her day in the hair salons, two kids running around in Gap denim, and a study filled with Civil War videos and Bette Midler records. An accountant's life.

Mortimer asked, "What are your plans for the holiday?"

"Nothing really." Fuddle donned one of the aprons. His woolen green tie clashed with the orange color of the smock.

"Going to spend it with the family?"

Fuddle stepped forward and took Mortimer's tongs from his hand.

"You've been here long enough," Fuddle said. "Why don't you get home to that nice girlfriend of yours?"

Mortimer hardly knew what to make of the manager's generosity. He didn't want to go home especially, but one did not refuse such a gracious offer. Mortimer handed over the utensil to Fuddle and removed his work apron, hanging it on one of the hooks by the Amsterdam Avenue entrance.

"Merry Christmas," Mortimer said.

Fuddle steeped behind the counter. He looked peculiar there. He was quite short and barely could be seen above the grill. With his big head and eyeglasses he looked rather like a frog with a pair of tongs.

He gave Mortimer a weak smile. "Merry Christmas to you," he said.

12.

On the first meeting of Biology 235: Introduction to Evolutionary Biology, in September 1990, Professor Fillmore Skinny posed the following questions: "What separates man from other animals? What makes humans human?"

Hands shot up.

"Ability to speak."

"Ability to reason."

"Guns."

"The New Kids on the Block." This was a popular musical group at the time, a joke. Most people have forgotten the New Kids, but at the time their immortality seemed assured.

Professor Skinny wrote all of the answers on a green chalkboard at the front of the lecture hall, arranging the responses into logical groupings: language, art, agriculture, self-destructive behavior, and so forth. By the time the class had exhausted itself the list had grown to an impressive size, two dozen or so items in all. He then dismissed the students without another word.

At the next meeting of the class, the chalkboard remained in its place on the stage. Skinny entered, wearing a tattered brown suit and bow tie—his customary costume—and pointed to the first word on the list: "language."

"Vervets," he said. "Vervets are a cat-sized breed of African monkey. They talk. When vervets see a leopard, the males give off a loud series of barks and the females squeal a high-pitched chirp. In response, all of the monkeys in the vicinity scramble up trees. When a vervet sees a martial eagle—the leading killer of vervets—it emits a short cough of two syllables. Nearby monkeys look up or run into the bush. If a vervet sees a dangerous snake, it chutters, and the vervets in the area stand on their hind legs and look down.

"Their vocabulary doesn't end here. Vervets have words for baboons, jackals, hyenas, and unfamiliar humans. When vervets interact with other vervets, they grunt. They have different grunts for when they approach dominant monkeys and subordinate monkeys, and for when they see a rival troop. They have a vocabulary of at least a dozen different words, and these are only the ones that scientists have been able to decipher so far.

"But animals don't have grammar, you say. Well, dolphins do. Marine biologists have trained dolphins to recognize symbols for dozens of nouns and verbs. They have also taught them linguistic instructions, like ignoring the previous word in a sentence. For example, say this to a trained dolphin: 'Bring hoop delete ball' and the dolphin will bring the ball instead of the hoop.

"Research in humans shows that the ability to learn language is genetically determined. People with a defect on the eleventh chromosome suffer from an affliction called Williams Syndrome. These people have rich vocabularies and something resembling an addiction to using flowery speech. Ask them to think of an animal and they will more likely pick an egret or an antelope than a cat or a dog. But they are severely retarded.

"People with a different defect on chromosome II suffer from something known as specific language impairment. They can memorize grammatical rules, but they cannot apply them instinctively. They know by heart that the plural of 'dog' is 'dogs,' but ask them the plural of an unfamiliar word, like chiropodist, and they're stuck. Passive voice, suffixes, word choice rules, all give them problems too. And it's entirely hereditary.

"So if animals other than humans have language and if the human ability to speak is genetically programmed, then this doesn't really belong on the list, does it? If anything, the evidence suggests that humans are more like other animals than not. It suggests instead that other animals have sophisticated linguistic capabilities, more sophisticated than we like to believe, and that it is only a matter of time before we comprehend these capacities better. The evidence certainly does not suggest that humans are unique in any way."

With that Professor Skinny walked over to the chalkboard and unceremoniously drew a line through the word "language." Then he walked out of the room.

So it went throughout the semester. The chalkboard never moved from its place at the front of the lecture hall. Each day Professor Skinny pointed to a different item on the list. Each day he explained how the type of behavior in question had a direct analogue in other animal behavior and the overwhelming evidence that it had been genetically programmed.

It was quite a disheartening process watching him dispose of all of the characteristics that people think of as uniquely human. One especially depressing day he tackled the subject of human personality. "Perhaps this should not even have been on the list in the first place," he said. "We all know animals with personalities: friendly dogs, impatient cats, an antisocial bird. What makes human personality different, you say, is that we can choose to be how we are. Animals are how they are, but it is up to us to shape our own temperament. Is it?

"Monkeys that are dominant in their social group have high levels of a chemical called serotonin. They are not especially big or fierce, as you might think. They are levelheaded, less impulsive than ordinary monkeys, less likely to interpret play as aggression. Monkeys with low levels of serotonin are more likely to be aggressive and ill-tempered.

"Scientists have studied serotonin levels in CEOs and fraternity presidents. Guess what they found? People in leadership positions have higher serotonin levels than their subordinates. People with low levels of serotonin are more likely to be aggressive and ill-tempered.

"Both monkeys and people can be manipulated. Low cholesterol diets reduce serotonin levels. Monkeys fed low-cholesterol diets become forty percent more likely to take aggressive action against a fellow monkey. Humans given cholesterol-lowering drugs become more violent too. They are far more likely to die from suicide or murder. Cholesterol treatment is a two-edged sword. It cuts the risk of a heart attack by fourteen percent, but it increases the risk of violent death by seventy-eight percent.

"Chemicals control every type of human behavior you can think of. Dopamine dictates motivation. People with low dopamine levels lack initiative. People with lots of dopamine ride motorcycles and jump out of airplanes. A neurotransmitter called norepinephrine stimulates the metabolism. It also makes people shy and apathetic. Scandinavians have lots of it. It helps them to withstand the cold.

"Each one of these different chemicals can be regulated. Doctors do it every day to treat everything from depression to schizophrenia to all sorts of compulsive behavior. People do it for themselves. Cocaine stimulates the release of dopamine, fatty foods the release of serotonin.

"So you say, all this proves is that there are lots of chemicals that affect human personality. What news is this? Everyone knows that each person has a predisposition to act in one way or the other. But what does this prove? What matters more is the environment in which they are raised. No matter how any person is born, he can be raised to be anyone or anything. Nurture matters more than nature, right? Well, consider this: A Harvard psychologist studied shyness in children. He found that he could identify shy types by as early as four months, and could predict how shy or confident these babies would grow up to be as adults. That's before the babies learned to talk, before they interacted with other children. They can't even see or hear very well at that age, and yet their personality had already been formed. Studies of twins, children of immigrants, adoptees all show the same thing: people get their personality from their genes, not their environment.

"You want to believe that your personality is your own. You think some things about yourself are distinctively your own, such as your clothes, the decorations in your dorm room, who your friends are. Genes don't determine these tastes, you say. For each of these things, answer me this: who chose them? Do you like Coca-Cola because it is better or because advertising has made you believe it tastes better or because evolution has conditioned you to seek sweet foods that give quick energy boosts? Do those of you who smoke do so because you have made the choice that nicotine addiction is good for you or can you just not stop and not even remember the reasons you started, maybe because your friends did it, or because it looked cool? Where do your conceptions of beauty come from? Do you look for people with good qualities? Or do you find yourself drawn to men and women in magazines and movies, people who don't even look like that in real life, for reasons you can't explain? Have you ever once in your life said to yourself 'I should like this' and succeeded in teaching yourself to like it? Not to tolerate it, but to genuinely like it?

"Who is in control?

"Who are you?"

Then he crossed personality from the board.

One by one they fell.

Art. "New Guinean bowerbirds," he said. "They build circular huts, as big as eight feet in diameter and four feet in height, with lawns of green moss decorated with flowers and fruits and leaves, all grouped together by color—reds with reds, blues with blues. They are magnificent, manicured with a degree of care that any lawn-mowing suburban husband would envy. Why do they do it? To attract mates. Female bowerbirds choose their companions by the quality of their bowers. Different for humans, you say. It's about the art, for us, the aesthetics. Is it? Listen to rock and roll musicians talk about why they got into music. They all give the same answer: girls. Maybe later it means more to them. But that's later."

Agriculture. "Leaf-cutter ants. They cut off leaves and slice them into pieces, which they use to cultivate fungus in their underground nests. They manure the leaves with ant saliva and feces and seed the leaves with their favorite fungus. As if they are weeding a garden, they remove the growth of any foreign species that crops up on their farm. When a queen goes to start a new colony, she carries with her a culture of the fungus, like a farmer taking seeds to the New World.

"Some ants keep cows. They feed on the sweet secretion of a variety of bugs—aphids and mealybugs, caterpillars and spittle insects. In exchange for the honeydew, the ants protect their cattle from predators and parasites. Some aphids have evolved to exist quite comfortably in this life; they are rather like domestic cattle. They have no defense mechanisms of any kind. They excrete the honeydew through their anus with a uniquely evolved mechanism that allows them to hold the sweet drop in place while an ant drinks it up. To stimulate the syrupy flow, the ants stroke the aphids with their antennae."

Self-destructive behavior. "Humans flaunt their smoking of cigarettes and consumption of alcohol. Surely, you say, they are alone in the glorification of this self-destructive behavior. Are they any different than a male bird of paradise, which grows a tail three feet long, or a long plume from its eyebrows, to attract a mate, even though the showy features are just as likely to attract a hawk? Both flaunt what they have, both publicly damage themselves, as if to say my genes are so strong that I can do this and still function well. Is one any different from the other? Is it rational to smoke? Is it rational to maintain a three-foot tail?"

So it went, day after day, week after week. Along the way, Skinny pointed out many disturbing things. One day he brought in a photograph of a chicken. The chicken's feathers had been cut and its thighs tied behind its ears, in the way they are sometimes sold in butcher shops. The picture had been taken from underneath the chicken, so its head was not visible. One could not tell what type of animal it was. He juxtaposed this against a photograph of a human being, similarly shorn, taken from the same angle.

It was hard to tell which was the chicken.

And which was the human.

He brought in pictures of human fetuses at different stages of development. At three weeks, the embryo most closely resembles a worm. At four, it has gills and webbed hands and looks decidedly reptilian. To make the comparison more striking, he placed the human pictures against photographs of animal embryos at similar stages of development. It was virtually impossible to tell the human embryo apart from the embryo of a pig or a rabbit or an elephant. It is only in the last few weeks of development, the last ten percent of the gestation period, that the fetus looks distinctively human.

The pictures drew groans from the students. They did not enjoy looking at chicken rumps or thinking about the fact that they once looked like lizards while inside their mothers' wombs. But this seemed to please Skinny all the more. He relished their moans of protest, went to great lengths to offend their sensibilities.

But nothing pleased him quite so much as crossing another item off the board. He performed this task with a flourish and conspicuous glee, as if he were vanquishing an especially hated enemy. And vanquish the enemy he did. One after the other the items disappeared from the list, fallen soldiers in a bloodless war. Skinny systematically savaged them, with his mind and a stick of chalk. He dispensed of them all, until only a single item remained.

Love.

13.

Epiphanies come at strange times—in the bathtub, under apple trees, at Irish family dinners. Mortimer Coleridge's came during a showing of the movie *Executive Sweets*. *Executive Sweets* tells the story of a young woman who advances her way through office politics by having sex with several of the men and women who work in the office, individually and in various combinations. She is quite a beautiful woman, far more attractive than the men in her office could ever hope to bed on their own merits. They all have bad mustaches and potbellies. Out of gratitude, they help the young woman advance up the corporate ladder.

In Mortimer's favorite scene, the young woman, Morgan, is working late in her office one evening when the custodian enters. She and the custodian strike up a conversation.

"What's your name?" Morgan asks.

"Jed," says the boy. "What's yours?"

"Morgan. Did you just start here?"

"Last week." An awkward stare passes between them before the boy goes about his work, dusting the table and cleaning Morgan's wastebasket. Despite her long day of work, the bin is empty.

"You don't seem to have any trash," he says. "Are there any

other jobs I can help you with?"

Morgan lifts her eyebrows mischievously and juts her chest. "I can think of one or two." A moment later the two are entwined. They kiss briefly, but Morgan doesn't care much for this perfunctory foreplay. In a matter of seconds she has loosed him and is fondling and groping. Soon he is upon her. Music begins to play in the background, a simple melody performed on an electric piano accompanied by synthesized drums.

Morgan's interest in the janitor is inconsistent from a dramatic perspective. To that point, she has shown interest only in people with the power to advance her career—her supervisor, an accountant for the company, an important shareholder. This boy cannot help her. He is nothing more than a janitor, perhaps not even a college graduate. Morgan has previously used sex only for power. This could only be explained as a dalliance. The scene might arguably be understood as suggesting that even the most sophisticated and driven of men and women are still at their core machines manufactured with the same basic functions: to eat and mate. This would be a sophisticated philosophical point. Mortimer liked to think that the director had intended to imply this, but he could not be sure.

In any event, at the climactic moment the janitor withdraws from Morgan's birth canal and expels his ejaculant on her face and breasts. He does this to frustrate the nucleic acids. For their purposes, it is critical that the seminal vesicles of the male be discharged directly into the sex organs of the woman. Otherwise procreation is not possible and hence no more nucleic acids can be made. From the acids' standpoint, the janitor's act is pure folly. They would not have approved.

Mortimer did though. He liked it very much. He liked the entire scene very much.

It was while watching this scene for the approximately two hundredth time that he had his epiphany.

Violet was underneath him, face down, hands against the cocktail table—black and rickety, one of those prefabricated affairs from IKEA—feet pressed for balance against the sleeper sofa. This made it possible for Mortimer to watch the movie while performing the act of lovemaking at the same time. Over the years Mortimer and Violet had tried several other methods, but none were quite as satisfying. This position required Violet to sustain a fair amount of weight on her arms. The couch had become worn in the place where she braced herself, and sometimes its metallic frame dug into the pads of her feet. It was grossly uncomfortable but she liked that it gave Mortimer pleasure. Though Mortimer did not see it this way, it was an accommodation for him.

She made many accommodations for him.

One accommodation she was not willing to make, however, was to allow Mortimer to discharge his seminal vesicles in the manner of the boy janitor. She preferred that he complete the coitus in a more traditional manner. She did, however, take a pill each day that tricked her body into thinking that she was perpetually pregnant. In a different manner, this also frustrated the nucleic acids.

Morgan and the janitor were nearing the climactic moment in the scene when Violet muttered her complaint. Mortimer knew the entire sequence of events in the movie by heart. The boy would let out three groans. Morgan would declare that she wanted the boy to ejaculate. He would then announce that he intended to ejaculate. Then he would ejaculate.

Mortimer did not hear Violet at first. He was heavily involved in the movie. She repeated herself.

"You're hurting me," she said.

This perturbed Mortimer. He had explained to her many times before that conversation interfered with his ability to become absorbed in the moment. Generally she obliged and refrained from saying anything during the act. Now it would take some concentration for him to finish.

"What is it?"

"You're pressing into me with your knee."

"Well what do you want me to do?" asked Mortimer, annoyed. How else did she expect him to do this?

"Just shift over a little bit to your left."

He did. She became quiet again for a while. He held out some small hope of getting it done. He checked the timer on the VCR: he still had four minutes and twelve seconds left. He liked to finish at the same time as the boy and he had a thing about watching the scene in its entirety, from start to finish. He could do it, but he felt some pressure. He bore down.

"You're still pressing into my knee."

Mortimer shifted once more; he was growing impatient.

She spoke again. "Do you think we could try it another way?" she asked.

Mortimer let out a heavy sigh. Could she possibly think this was the right time for this? If she were going to insist on having a conversation they would never be able to get through it. Exasperated, Mortimer reached with his hand for the VCR control, stopped the movie and turned off the television. Violet righted herself and sat down upon the couch. He looked at her.

"How do you want to do it?"

"I don't know," she said. "Some way that I can see you."

"You know we've tried that before." They had, many times, without success. He would get tired, she would become sore. It was nothing personal against Violet. She just, as they say, didn't do it for him. Nothing helped except the accommodation they had reached. She knew this, yet still she insisted.

"Can't we try it again," she said. "Maybe it will be different this time. It feels so impersonal this way."

Mortimer took her hand in his. "It's not impersonal," he said. "It's not any different than what every other two people in the world do. Screwing is always about an image. You don't have sex with another person, you have sex with some mental picture you have of the other person. That mental picture always differs a bit from the reality. When you close your eyes and think of the other person, they are always a little more beautiful or handsome than they are in real life. Maybe you remember what they looked like when you first met, when they were twenty pounds lighter, or how they looked on some night you went dancing or for some romantic dinner. Maybe you imagine being with them in another setting, or with another person, or maybe you even imagine them to be someone else.

"It's the same way with love. You don't fall in love with another person, you fall in love with what that person makes you feel about yourself—attractive, virile, needed. How they look doesn't matter, it only matters how they make you appear to yourself. 'People will see me with this person and they will take another look at me. They will look closer and see the beauty that they have never seen before. They will envy me.'

"Romance, love, sex—it's all mutual masturbation. You and I are just honest about it. We've dropped the pretenses."

Mortimer smiled when he finished and, for a moment, thought that he had gotten through to her. He believed most of what he said. He certainly believed it was true for most people. If he had been completely candid he would have modified his statement only by adding that he also believed that some love could transcend these constraints, that some people who truly understood each other could soar to new heights, achieve bliss not known by ordinary men. This was not the kind of love that he and Violet had, though he did not say this of course. She understood that what existed between them was an accommodation. More accurately, Mortimer believed or hoped that Violet understood this. He peered anxiously into her face, hoping to find some sign of understanding.

Instead he found only supplication. She pleaded with her eyes.

"Please," she said. "It's Christmas Day. Just this once."

His heart sunk.

Mortimer obliged her. He felt some sense of duty. She was a good girl, sweet and generous, not the person for him, but he could recognize her positive traits. And she had been kind to him, supportive of his work, indulgent of his idiosyncrasies. Her happiness was not his first aim, but he also did not desire her to be unhappy. And he knew what would happen if he refused her. There would be tears, endless tears, and talk of her mother. This he could not bear.

He steeled himself and tried his best. She knew some things he liked. She was a smart girl, sensitive to his body. But it wasn't enough. He felt nothing.

He could begin to feel Violet growing frustrated. Soon she would start to cry.

He conjured up an image in his mind, one he had used before, of himself and his love together at the top of a mountain, a tall, isolated mountain in the Andes that he had seen in a movie. There was not a person to be found within miles. The world was theirs. He felt the cool moss on his back. The wind gusted around them. She shed her clothes and shook her head. The wind blew through it like a mane. She embraced the breeze, stretching her arms to their full length and closing her eyes. Her skin tightened in the breeze. He had never seen anyone more beautiful in his life. She was free, completely free. And she wanted only him. They made love there on the mountain, there at the top of the world. Ecstasy.

This was enough to get him aroused. He mounted her. Violet sighed.

"Isn't this better?" she said.

Mortimer said nothing. Facing Violet in this way, he could not help but take notice of her body. With her legs splayed she looked rather like the slide of the chicken Professor Skinny had displayed in class. Mortimer tried desperately to hold the image of the mountain in his mind.

"This is what love should be. Love shouldn't be suffering."

Mortimer didn't hear the words at first. He had been concentrating too intently on his fantasy. Violet's voice interfered with this. He needed to imagine that she was not there. But her words broke through. They annoyed him. If she was going to insist upon this, the least she could do was not to demand conversation also. And then what she had said seeped into his consciousness. The words got him thinking, the spark of an idea that seemed to merit further consideration.

He slowed down.

"Did you hear what I said?" she asked.

He didn't hear the question. The idea began to ignite in his mind, neurons firing one after the other. The pieces came together like a jigsaw puzzle. It all made sense now. How had he not seen it before?

"Are you okay?" she asked.

He reached with his hand to the end table behind her head and retrieved his notebook, which was nearby, as always.

Violet became more desperate. "What's going on?" she asked.

"What happened? What did I do wrong?" She began to weep quiet tears, the pathetic cry of a child who believes it has failed but does not entirely understand why.

Mortimer did not notice. He had already started writing.

14.

From the journal of Mortimer Taylor Coleridge

The answer should have been obvious. Now that I have seen it, I wonder how it ever was obscure. It is often this way with grand ideas, I suppose. We look back and wonder how we ever did not know.

The irony is that Gwen herself held the answer all the while. All I had to do was look in front of me. It is often this way too, I suppose.

It is easy to think, looking at her now, that it was always this way, that the spotlights of heaven always shined upon her as if her success had been predestined, but this is not the case. In the beginning she was not the woman she is today. In the beginning she suffered.

Her band did not make it at first. After the suicide, they stayed together, playing clubs and house parties in the Anaheim area. They became popular with the local youth. In 1991, a record company signed them to a contract. The next year they released their first album. The songs sounded good, but they were not about much of anything at all. One, "Ache," told about the extraction of wisdom teeth:

He was a well-educated man, had his degree in medicine
I noticed his hairy hands. . . he was a very, very hairy man

He looked right down in, shook his head and then
Said "these teeth must be pulled right away!"

The album did not sell well. The band went on tour to promote the record. Few people attended the concerts.

No Doubt spent the next two years in music purgatory. Their record label withdrew its support. It refused to pay for tours or for promotion of the album. The environment was not ripe for ska, they said. These were the days of grunge, a dark and dour kind of music with loud guitar and mumbled lyrics that could barely be heard at all. The songs seemed to have words only because the bands were told the songs had to have words. This quasi-musical grousing was Seattle's gift to the world in the 1990s. This and expensive coffee.

Left on its own, No Doubt independently released a collection of songs that had not made it onto their first album, including "Total Hate," a song written by John Spence before his death. This is the chorus to "Total Hate":

Total Hate
Total Hate
Total Hate
Total Hate

To this point, Gwen had played only a contributing role in the artistic development of the band. She was the lead singer, of course, and she wrote or helped to write several songs for each of the albums, but it was mostly her brother's band. Everyone seemed content with this arrangement.

Through this all, the suicide and the down years, Gwen had a relationship with the band's bass player, Tony Kanal. It began after band practice one day. Gwen approached the boy, a year younger than she, and asked when he planned to kiss her. It started just like that.

They were guarded about the relationship at first. Tony felt he had broken an unspoken rule against dating the bandleader's sister. They only revealed the relationship later, some time after John Spence's death. Everyone accepted it. Whatever reservations they may have had, they could see that Tony and Gwen loved each other. The couple spent every moment together.

Then, in 1993, he broke up with her.

The news sent Gwen reeling. She had believed they would marry. Now, as if things could be any worse, she faced the prospect of having to remain in a band with the man she had once loved.

She despaired.

But something else happened, something profound and wonderful: she began to write about her experiences, powerful, heartfelt words, poetry:

You see it's hard to face
The addict that's inside of me
I want to fill my glass up
With you constantly

She wrote about her anger with astonishing realism:

You killed the pair
Now only one is breathing
There's no looking back

"Are you happy now?" she asks, over and over, berating her ex-lover. At the end of the song she taunts him: "You're by yourself. All by yourself. You have no one else. You're by yourself." The listener can't help but shake his or her head and wince just a little bit. It is clear that this is a real person singing. These are real feelings. People related to the honesty of the songs.

The band's independent release, *The Beacon Street Collection*, sold fewer than 100,000 copies. The next album, *Tragic Kingdom*, the first album in which Gwen asserted her artistic influence, sold more than fourteen million. Most people could not comprehend the issues that she raised in her songs: the quest for meaning, doubts about whether we can master ourselves, about whether we really possess free will. But even the average person had some intuitive sense that this music was somehow different from pedestrian popular music, that this person asked questions that mattered to everyone.

They flocked to the music. They flocked to her.

But this great art was born of great suffering. In the early days of No Doubt, Gwen had it all: the man she loved, a sense of purpose. And the band made songs about dentists and trains. But when she was shaken to her core, made to doubt everything she believed, led to the fountain of despair, then things began to happen. When she was forced to ask the question that has nagged at man since he became aware of his own existence—what does it all mean?—then and only then, did the muse sing.

The answer was there all the while. Only those that suffer can achieve greatness. This is the single path that must be followed.

She showed the way.

I know now what I must do.

SECOND STANZA

Most people, Kamala, are like a falling leaf that drifts and turns in the air, flutters and falls to the ground. But a few others are like stars which travel one defined path: no wind reaches them, they have within themselves their guide and path.

– Siddartha

15.

Mortimer and Garcia sat at a booth at the Nathan's on the corner of 108th and Broadway. Garcia had his hot dog with mustard and sauerkraut, Mortimer plain, with a dab of relish on the side. Garcia drank lemonade; Mortimer drank water he carried in a bottle from home. He knew the mark up on lemonade.

The two men occasionally had lunch together, always Mortimer's treat because Garcia did not have much money. He had six kids at home and they didn't pay enough at the Papaya Queen to support a family of even half that size. Most days, Garcia had Papaya Queen for lunch since employees could buy franks for a quarter each. Mortimer did this too, usually. But it was good to break the cycle sometimes—to get out and about—and, besides, Mortimer needed to talk.

"I feel bad about it, but what am I supposed to do?" Mortimer asked. "I have to prepare myself, and this is the first step."

Garcia had mustard on the side of his mouth. Mortimer gestured towards it with his hand. Garcia wiped the mustard away then bit again into his hot dog. He had a ravenous appetite; it always seemed as if he had not eaten for days.

"I know she's a good person," Mortimer continued. "She's sweet and kind and gentle. It's really quite remarkable given everything that she has been through. And she could not be more thoughtful of me. Some people say that she is better than I have a right to expect. They do. I know they do."

Mortimer looked up from the table. Garcia had a speckle of lemonade on his nose. Mortimer gestured again with his hand. Garcia wiped.

"Gracias," he said, his mouth full of frank. In many ways, Garcia was the perfect person with whom to share this story. He had been married at seventeen, after he had gotten his girlfriend pregnant in the back seat of an El Dorado. For his entire adult life Garcia had known only responsibility: a wife, six kids by the age of twenty-five. He worked like a dog to support them all and never once complained. But Mortimer knew Garcia would understand the fire raging in his own heart. Sometimes, late in the evenings, Garcia and Cecilia, one of the counter girls, would sneak into Mr. Fuddle's office for a minute or two. The flame of passion still burned inside Garcia.

"I know she's a wonderful person," Mortimer continued, "but I also know that she's not the person for me. She is happy at heart, an optimist. She can find the good in anything. She's a Catholic, you know. They have a way with that. A plane crashes, some kid dies of leukemia and they just smile and say that it's all for the best, all part of God's will. It's a useful belief, but not one that we share.

"We want different things. She wants children and a house with a lawn for me to mow on weekends. She's happy to watch television and eat macaroni and cheese.

"She really likes macaroni and cheese.

"Now don't get me wrong, there's nothing wrong with any of that. I'm not judging. But it's not what I want. I embrace all of the bitter pills that life gives us to swallow. I don't want to explain them away blithely. I want to immerse myself in them, to try to understand, to try to find meaning. I don't want a life of television and noodles. I want a searching life, a life of books and music and philosophy.

"I want more.

"Do you know what I mean?"

Garcia said, "Sí." He had a sliver of sauerkraut caught between his incisor and bicuspid. Mortimer let it go.

"Am I just supposed to settle? Is this what people do in the end? Do they just resign themselves to a less than happy existence because some relationship is better than none or because the other person is the best that they think they can do? When fathers talk to sons before weddings, do they say, 'I know you're having second thoughts, and you should, because chances are you won't end up very happy. In all probability you'll end up like your mother and me, two people without love for one another who live together as—for want of a better word—an accommodation. Most likely you will be unhappy. But it's a different sort of unhappiness than being alone, probably not as bad, though I can't be sure since I haven't experienced the other and won't, God willing. But it probably is worse. It almost certainly is since so many people choose to avoid it. And in any case, if you call things off now, you'll hurt her feelings real bad, and she's a nice girl, so you probably should go through with it.'

"Is this what fathers say to their sons?

"Is this the way people think?"

Garcia said nothing. He had finished his food, and just sat there now, quietly, waiting for Mortimer to spend himself. Garcia had penetrating green eyes. They burned their attention on the hot dog sitting on the paper cradle in front of Mortimer. Mortimer had not touched the frankfurter; he was too engaged in the conversation. He pushed it across the table. Garcia nodded thanks and tore into it.

"Maybe that is what people say," said Mortimer, "but that's not for me.

"It's like I've been given this once in a lifetime opportunity, a glimpse of heaven, a chance to pull for the brass ring. This could be the storybook ending that people dream about, the stuff they see on movies and television.

"I know that the odds are long. She's a rock star and I'm a hot dog guy. She's beautiful and I'm nothing to speak of. I know everything about her; she knows nothing about me. But I also know that we understand each other. I've never felt a stronger connection to someone. We're asking the same questions, we want the same things out of life.

"That's still no guarantee, I know, but I can improve the odds. I can improve myself. I can make myself stronger and more centered. I can make myself more disciplined, so that the man that she eventually meets will not just be extraordinary on the inside, but extraordinary on the outside too. I understand the importance of the package. I shall improve the package so that when the day does come, the chance that she will notice is maximized.

"It is still a chance, I know, but it's one I have to take. I can't just accept a mediocre life when I have a chance for the sublime. I have to fly to the sun, even if I burn out trying, like a modern-day Icarus. Otherwise I will regret it for the rest of my life, both for what it cost me and for what it cost her.

"It's also about her. Don't forget that. I owe it to her too.

"Do you know what I mean?"

Garcia stared back at Mortimer, his eyes blinking slowly. He should not have eaten the third hot dog. He felt sleepy now, and bloated. He wanted badly for Mortimer to stop talking so he could put his head down and take a nap, but he didn't feel right about doing it in the middle of the story. After all, Mortimer had bought him lunch.

Garcia could not understand much of what Mortimer was saying. His English was spotty. Something about Violet and a wedding. This pleased Garcia. He liked Violet. She was a pretty girl, better than Mortimer should have been able to attract. Back at the Papaya Queen, Garcia and his friends referred to Mortimer as *El Guapo*, which is loosely translated as "The Handsome One."

They were being ironic, of course. Mortimer was smart to keep Violet.

His eyelids heavy, Garcia nodded his head compassionately.

"Sí," he said.

Mortimer smiled.

"I knew you would understand," he said.

16.

It seemed pathetic sitting there on the green chalkboard, all by itself. A solitary sentry guarding an abandoned bunker, a last soldier in a lost war. A single word was all that remained of the distinctiveness of humanity: "love."

The number of students filling the rows of seats in the old classroom had dwindled over the course of the semester. Fillmore Skinny did not take attendance and had a reputation for asking vague essay questions on his exams, the sort that one could answer by doing just a little bit of the course reading or even from life experience alone. Legend had it that one spring Skinny asked but a lone question on his final exam: "What is the meaning of life?" Less than two minutes after the distribution of the blue books, a student turned in his exam to the proctor. He wrote: "It is far too nice a day to contemplate the meaning of life."

He received an "A" from Professor Skinny.

Most people received A's from Professor Skinny. Hence the nickname of the class, "Apes," as it was universally known among the Columbia student body, came to describe the students that chose the class as much as the subject matter of the course. As it became clear over the course of the Spring 1990 semester that

Professor Skinny would be no more demanding than he had been in years past, students dropped from the seats like flies. They would cram a little on the night before the final and fake their way through the exam by writing about the weather.

By the last lecture, only a few scattered souls remained: some geeks who feared that this would be the year that Skinny would surprise the students with a tough exam, some high achievers whose moral sense would not allow them to duck class, and some vagrants who wandered in off the streets to get the benefit of a free Columbia education or just to get out of the cold. Smallest of all was the group to which Mortimer Taylor Coleridge belonged—those who saw Fillmore Skinny not as a codger or a buffoon to be exploited for an easy A, but as an oracle, the rare great professor who changed the very way one looked at the world. This was a group of precisely one. Mortimer sat rapt as Skinny spoke his final words of the semester.

"What about love?" Skinny asked. He paced about the stage, letting the question linger in the air. It reverberated against the wooden rafters and seats of the old lecture hall. Early in the semester, students had filled these seats, dampening his words. They were gone now, and the question echoed back and forth.

"It's oxytocin mostly, a hormone released by both males and females during orgasm.

"The males of a Midwestern breed of a little mouse-like mammal called voles are fiercely loyal. They mate for life and never cheat. Northwestern voles are philanderers, tramps. When scientists examined the brains of the Midwestern voles, they found that they had oxytocin receptors in the pleasure centers of their brains. The Northwestern voles have their oxytocin centers in an entirely different part of the brain, an area associated with aggressive behavior.

"People with lots of oxytocin form relationships easily. People with too little have anxiety about forming close bonds. In one study, scientists examined a group of students each of whom described himself as being madly in love. The scientists hooked these students up to brain-imagining equipment. When the scientists showed the smitten students pictures of their loved ones, blood rushed to four small sections of the brain, areas rich with receptors for oxytocin and our old friend dopamine.

"Study after study shows that romantic infatuation lasts no more than two or three years. The chemicals associated with a new love have less and less of an impact on the body over time, in the same way that the body builds tolerance to a drug or resistance to a disease. Love is a disease. Call it a condition if this makes you feel any better about it. It reduces productivity and impairs decision-making ability. We all recognize this intuitively. We excuse impetuous action on the basis that someone is under the influence of love.

"You say that at least we can choose who we love. This is what makes it special. Do we? Do we choose it or does it choose us? Psychologists have some interesting data to offer. They have looked at thousands of married couples, examining everything conceivable about them, with an eye to figuring out how people make some choices. Some of what they found won't surprise you. The biggest correlations are between people with similar religions and racial and socioeconomic backgrounds. This makes sense, you say. People with these big things in common are more likely to be happy together. It's good that they steer themselves in this way.

"But are they steering or being steered? Race and religion aren't the only predictive factors. On average, people tend to pick partners that look like themselves, not just in height and weight and eye color, but for all sorts of characteristics that you would never suspect: earlobe length, wrist circumference, lung volume. The single biggest predictive factor in picking partners is length of middle finger. People tend to pick partners who have relatively long or short middle fingers, like their own.

"What should this say to us? People pick their lovers on the basis of a whole host of traits of which they are not conscious. Think about your own experience. Do you choose your lovers impassively or do you wake up one morning to find yourself drowning in emotion, out of control? Have you ever once succeeded in telling yourself whom you should love? Perhaps you've stayed with a boyfriend or girlfriend longer than you otherwise might have because you thought they were kind or responsible, but have you ever once kept your heart from wandering? Have you ever been able to tell it what it should want?

"In light of this, does it even make sense to think of love as a choice? Are we rational actors, choosing stoically among the host of would-be partners in the world? Who will make us most happy? Who understands us the best? We work from a model in making our way through the thousands upon thousands of choices. But do we make the model? Do we lie in our beds contemplating the ideal man or woman to suit our needs? Or is the model pre-formed? We speak of someone as our type. Who makes the type? Are we the masters or the puppets?

"If it is not a choice, then what is love? If our genes tell us whom to love, is love worthy of poetry and song? If it is nothing more than a surge of hormones, if we can control it no more than we can control our hunger or our need to breathe, what sense does it make to romanticize it?

"You students will tell me it is different somehow. You always do. But is it?"

He walked over to the blackboard then, as he had dozens of times throughout the semester; the eight remaining students and bums in the class drew their collective breath as he prepared to deliver the deathblow. And the professor, who reveled in disconcerting his charges, unsettled them once more. Fillmore Skinny picked up the chalk and next to the only uncrossed word on the board, "love", drew a question mark and walked out of the room.

17.

Violet did not take the news well. By his own admission, Mortimer could have come up with a better way to break it to the girl. But he neither had any experience in such matters, nor had he put much thought into how to handle it. He simply called her up one morning and said that she should drop by work that day because he had something to tell her.

She came, of course. She would have done anything for him and Mortimer had never made any similar request to talk, which worried her especially. It was a Thursday, which meant she had to take time off from work. Since she did not receive vacation time or sick leave, the time she missed at work cost her money. On the other hand, in his decade at Papaya Queen, Mortimer had accumulated nearly four months of compensatory leave through unused sick leave and overtime. He could easily have afforded to take the time off to visit her, but this act of consideration did not cross his mind.

She arrived around ten o'clock, less than an hour and a half after he had called, with a look of great concern on her face. Mortimer recognized her anxiety. He had seen it before when she fretted about some triviality or another, such as her mother's health or record store politics.

It was not busy at Papaya Queen when she got there. Late mornings were the lightest time—after the sale of sausage, egg and cheese sandwiches ebbed but before the lunchtime crowd started filing in. Merely half a dozen people were in the store, all stalwarts who could not wait until noon to satisfy their frankfurter cravings.

Mortimer made Violet wait nevertheless. Even after he saw her, Mortimer dealt patiently with the remaining customers in his line. Only after the line was cleared did he ask to be relieved. He stood solemnly in place, as if he were turning over the helm of a naval warship, until one of his colleagues, Garcia as it was, came to take his place. Only then did Mortimer acknowledge Violet's presence.

Throughout this charade, Violet waited patiently. She took his work seriously, so seriously that she indulged his belief that the sale of the world's greatest frankfurter was a mission more than a job. She would never have dared interrupt him while he was at work. Now that he had been relieved she rushed forward to meet him, grabbing him by the arm.

"Is everything okay?"

He brushed away her arm, conscious of the stares of his colleagues, and ushered her out the door.

"Let's talk outside." Mortimer had no desire for anyone to hear the conversation.

They stood to the right of the 110th Street entrance to the store, by the synagogue, out of the way of patrons. Winter had not yet set upon the city, but already it had turned cool, unseasonably so. The Columbia students passing by the store on their way to classes had already broken out their parkas and winter coats. They seemed dejected as they toted their knapsacks to school; the cold had come too soon.

Mortimer felt chilled himself. He wore only his work apron, with the words "Snappy Service" blazoned on the front right breast pocket. He kept a pen there, a Pilot Uniball Fine Point, for "precision writing, " as he always did, though he had never once had need of it in the store, other than to jot in his journal during breaks, and he always kept a pen fastened to the front cover of his journal anyway. The apron offered little protection against the cold. Violet did not have a coat either. In her haste to meet Mortimer she had forgotten to put one on. She shivered ever so slightly.

"I've fallen in love with someone else," Mortimer blurted out.

Violet did not say anything at first. She seemed not to understand the words, let alone to process the news.

"What do you mean?"

"What isn't clear about that?" Mortimer snapped. "I've fallen for somebody else. There's another woman."

"Somebody I know?"

"No one you know."

Violet nodded her head and turned away from Mortimer. She stared at the ground thinking about what he had said. To Mortimer it seemed as if this took quite a long time.

Finally, she spoke.

"I've done something wrong."

"You haven't done anything wrong."

"I've displeased you in some way."

"No."

"I must have," she said. Now her words gushed out. "I must have hurt you or made you mad or not done something I could have done. I've failed in some way. I must have, otherwise you wouldn't be feeling this way."

"You haven't done anything wrong."

"Just tell me what it is. I would do anything to make you happy. Just tell me."

"There isn't anything."

"But I love you," she said. Her eyes began to swell.

Mortimer saw the tears begin to pool. He wanted very much to keep them from flowing.

"You don't love me," he said, gently. "What you think of as love is just a craving, like your need for food or drink or air. You think it's somehow different than that, that's it's an emotion over which you have control, but it isn't. It's just another way that your body has been programmed. It tells you whom to want and when to want him. It's about sex and companionship and protection. It's about basic human needs. That isn't love. That's an itch that you have to scratch. What we commonly mistake for love is an animalistic thing.

"True love is something different entirely; it has nothing to do with any of these coarse desires. True love is a connection people make at the level that makes human beings different from other animals, at the level of reason. It is a connection between people who share common beliefs, an outlook on life, a connection between people who ask the same questions.

"True love is not about sex or attraction. It does not even require physical proximity for its consummation. This is because it is intellectual, not corporeal. What you feel isn't love. It's like lust or something that we do not have the vocabulary to describe, but it is not love."

She looked at him. "And you love this other woman?"

He could not lie.

"I do."

Violet began to sob uncontrollably. Her eyes became a fountain of tears; she made weeping noises that came from the back of her throat, so loud that she could barely breathe. They seemed unreal to Mortimer, a contrivance to manipulate someone into giving something desired. It was always this way with ordinary people, always about their needs. They could not help themselves. Still it bothered him. He would have given almost anything to make the tears stop.

As it happened, a man walked by then carrying a bouquet of roses, a kindly looking black man with gentle eyes and flecks of gray at his temples. Mortimer had seen him before. He stopped in the store from time to time, hocking his wares to unsuspecting students who could be shamed into buying a posy or two for their lady friends. He had even approached Mortimer once or twice, on his way to or from work. Mortimer had always ignored him; he had no need for such excesses.

Mortimer had wondered whether the man might be a vagrant. It was a bum's job selling things on the street. But the man did not look destitute. He wore a well-maintained overcoat and a tidy plaid cap that matched the jacket rather well. These were not the clothes of a banker, but they also did not bespeak of poverty. There was money in flowers, much more than in pencils or batteries or the other trinkets the itinerants sold on the streets and in the subways. The money was especially good with roses, which cost twenty-five cents or so wholesale, and might be sold in a store for ten or fifteen dollars a dozen, a good profit margin. Not as good as the margin on papaya drink, but good all the same.

By the time the man reached the store, Violet's tears had subsided a bit. She still cried steadily, but not so much that a passer-by could tell whether these were the tears of a broken heart or merely the aftermath of a minor tiff or, as Mortimer hoped despite its implausibility, tears of joy. The salesman angled his way over, tipped one of the roses forward out of the bunch, and placed it in Mortimer's hand.

"Pay me what you think is fair," he said. He always said the same thing.

Mortimer instinctively raised his hand to refuse the flower, but then thought better of it. In the six years they dated, he had never once bought Violet flowers or chocolate or anything of that sort. On one occasion she had made a point of this, during a spell of heightened insecurity. He explained at the time that she should not require such trifles to have confidence in his feelings for her. She never raised the subject again. Mortimer thought this might be an appropriate time for flowers. At the least it would be a nice gesture.

He reached into his pocket and pulled out a dollar bill. He handed the bill to the salesman and relieved him of the flower, which he then handed over to Violet. The salesman clutched the bill in his fist.

The flower nonplussed Violet. She turned it over in her hand, wondering at the significance of Mortimer's display of sensitivity at such a moment. He had never shown any such tenderness before. She wondered whether he might be having second thoughts, wondered whether there might still be some chance of salvaging their relationship.

Mortimer watched her for a moment. He understood that he should offer Violet his attention, but he became distracted by the salesman, who was still lingering in the vicinity. He was clutching the money Mortimer had paid him, yet refusing to look at what his clenched hand contained, as if it were a tiny birthday present, a surprise. Finally he relaxed his hand and checked the denomination of the bill. After he examined it he began to mutter invective under his breath. Mortimer could not discern all of it, but he clearly hears the words "cheap bastard." Furthermore, the salesman cast several dirty looks in Mortimer's direction, while continuing to loiter close by.

Oblivious to all of this, Violet continued to cry. Mortimer left her and walked over to the salesman.

"Is there a problem?" he asked.

The salesman muttered inaudibly and turned away.

Mortimer pressed forward.

"What is it? Do you have some kind of problem with me?"

"A buck, man. You gave me a buck."

"You said to pay what I thought was fair."

"But a buck, man?" The salesman shook his head.

"What do you think is fair?" Mortimer asked.

"I don't know. Five. Three. Two. Not a buck, though." He shook his head again. "No way a buck."

"If you thought two dollars was the fair price, why didn't you ask for it in the first place?"

"That's not the way I operate."

The salesman tried to retreat, but Mortimer forced himself upon him.

"You have a lot of nerve setting people up like that," he said. "If you have a price you want then you should ask for it rather than making people feel cheap when they don't give you what you want? What you're really doing is trying to get some sucker to give you way more than the flower is worth because he has no idea how much it is supposed to cost and because he doesn't want to look chintzy in front of his date. You have gall. You have infinite gall."

The salesman walked away, turning his back to Mortimer and gesturing with his hand that he wanted no more of the conversation, but Mortimer pressed on, following him down 110th Street, berating him about his questionable business practices, and offering a diatribe on the unconscionable mark-up on flowers.

Violet remained by the store, sobbing out of control. She keeled over in pain from the tears. When he exhausted himself with the salesman, Mortimer turned around and saw Violet in the distance. He saw too when Bertrand Fuddle walked out of the store and wrapped his coat around Violet and began walking her down Amsterdam Avenue, in the direction of his home.

Mortimer thought of going after them, but it seemed better to him to leave things as they were with Violet. And, besides, he had more important things on his mind.

18.

From the journal of Mortimer Taylor Coleridge

The album *Return of Saturn* explores in depth the question Fillmore Skinny raised in his last lecture: Can we control the yearnings of our heart? In "Ex-Girlfriend," Gwen talks of her love for a man whom she knew would inevitably hurt her. "I kinda always knew I'd end up your ex-girlfriend," she laments speaking of a man who is too wild and too free. She finds herself changing to suit him, and realizes that if they were meant for one another that change would not be required of her. She senses a dangerous pattern being repeated. "We keep repeating mistakes for souvenirs," she writes, and knows that she should know better. But once her heart has been touched, there can be no turning back. "I'm another ex-girlfriend on your list," she says. "But I should have thought of that before we kissed."

"Artificial Sweetener" addresses the issue from the reverse standpoint. Here, Gwen chastises herself for not loving someone that her rational self believes she should love. She finds herself "faking I love you's," to someone whom she intellectually regards as worthy of affection. "You really deserve love," she writes. "But I can't seem to find myself." She attempts, without success to ascertain why it is that she cannot return this love. She wonders whether she hesitates because she was born two weeks late or whether it is because she is stupid or stubborn. She does not know. The only thing she knows for sure is that she is not sure.

Over and over again she returns to the theme. "Simple Kind of Life" refers to the kind of life that she had wanted for herself when she was in love with the bass player from the band. In these days she dreamed about being a wife and a mother. Now she finds that—in spite of herself—she has become too faithful to her freedom. "A selfish kind of life," she calls it, when all she wanted before were the simple things, and a simple kind of life.

In "Bathwater," she muses yet again about her attraction to a man whom she rationally understands to be bad for her. She recognizes this man as a cassanova, someone who possesses a "museum of lovers." He is beautiful, the object of every woman's affection, and irrepressible, and she is insecure. In loving him she knows herself to be causing her own destruction. And still she pursues him. "Why do the good girls always want the bad boy?" she wonders, as she recognizes herself to be "choking" on all of her own contradictions.

Even the title of the album, referenced in "Artificial Sweetener," is itself an allusion to the impossibility of mastery over oneself. It derives from the 29 and one-half year period that Saturn takes to revolve around the Sun. The return of Saturn is regarded as a transformative moment in one's life, associated with the fear, doubt, and personal reflection that go hand in hand with maturity. It is one reason the thirtieth birthday is regarded as such a watershed moment in people's lives. Gwen herself was turning thirty around this time.

So it only makes sense that Gwen would have been thinking about these issues during the writing of *Return of Saturn*. And her life circumstances brought the issues even closer. Around this time she began dating a singer from a band with which No Doubt had been touring the country. One can only imagine the doubts she must have been feeling after the initial euphoria wore off. Her heart had just been broken by a man she dated for seven years, the man she believed she would marry. Now she found herself drawn to another rock musician. What sort of person could offer less stability than a man who tours the world with his musical troupe? Who could offer less security than someone who is the object of every woman's desire, someone for whom temptation waits in every city?

She knew all of this. And still she wanted him.

Why?

What is it?

Can it be mastered?

I know what you're thinking. It is not a problem. Gwen's relationship with this crooner does not bother me. To the contrary, it gives me great hope. It is good for her to get this out of her system. We all feel the need to date an actor or a rock star at some point in our lives, to have some intensely ego-gratifying relationship. Then we have it and we wonder whether this is all there is, whether there is more.

This is where she is now. Posing the questions that few men and women ever reach the level of awareness to ask. The questions that I can help her answer.

19.

After disposing of Violet, Mortimer purged himself of the remaining material items that tied him to his former life. He did not have much. Some essentials: a small refrigerator, a mattress, a twelve-inch television and VCR. Modest indulgences: a set of *Star Trek* coasters, a Cuisinart, a small but well used collection of pornographic videos. Mortimer loaded all of it into a U-Haul and carted the lot from his apartment in Washington Heights to a pawnshop on Jerome Avenue in the Bronx called Lucky's Pawn.

The sign above the front door of the pawnshop had a picture of a chess piece. It was supposed to be a pawn, of course, but it was actually a rook. The sign maker's assistant had made a mistake. He did not know one piece from the other. Rather than redo the sign, the sign maker took the chance that the pawnshop owner would not know the difference. He didn't. He did not know that the castle was a powerful piece that could move across the board in either of two directions or that the pawn was a puny piece that could move only one or two squares. He had never played chess in his life.

This is what the sign said:

Lucky's Pawn

We Pay the "Best" Prices in the Bronx

Lucky himself wasn't in good shape. He could only breathe through a hole that had been cut into his trachea. Lucky had emphysema. When Mortimer entered the store, Lucky furtively extinguished a Lucky Strike cigarette that he had been inhaling through his breathing hole. Lots of things were hard for Lucky— he couldn't walk down the street without losing his breath, even eating was a struggle—but he could smoke as well as he ever had. Through the breathing hole the nicotine went straight to his lungs, unfiltered. He liked it even better than the old way.

Lucky did not smoke Lucky Strikes because of the brand name. In fact, it had gone exactly the opposite way. One day in a sports magazine he saw a photograph of a man on a horse roping cattle, a vigorous and athletic man—even under his thick flannel shirt the bulges of his muscles were visible—the sort of man that attracted women without effort. Out of the side of his mouth, dangling from his lower lip, hung a Lucky Strike cigarette.

Lucky started smoking Lucky Strikes the next day. He was fourteen. This was in 1948. Soon he became a dependable smoker. He did not like to be seen without a cigarette in his mouth; he regarded it as part of his image. His friends knew they could always count on him to bum a cigarette. They would say things like "Got a Lucky?" or "How 'bout a Lucky?" Eventually they shortened this to plain "Lucky." It was a question at first, later an arguably ironic statement as in "you're lucky," then finally just the name that had stuck with him since. His real name was Herman Purdy.

Lucky followed Mortimer out to the U-Haul. He emitted a

series of short phlegmy coughs as he sorted through Mortimer's things. Every so often he mumbled to himself, as if he were lost in thought. He held a pad and pencil in his hands, which he used to make occasional notes. All in all, he seemed to treat the matter quite solemnly.

After several minutes, Lucky looked up from his pad.

"Three hundred dollars," he said. Lucky spoke by blowing words out of his trachea tube. This took some getting used to.

"For what?" asked Mortimer.

"For all of it."

"You can't be serious."

"That's the best I can do."

Mortimer looked through his things. It felt strange to see everything he had ever owned lying on the floor of a rental van. It seemed like very little to show for thirty years.

"This is my entire life you're talking about," Mortimer said slowly. "You're offering only three hundred dollars for my entire life?"

"I can't put a price on a life," Lucky said. "I can only put a price on the bed and the TV." This left him out of breath. Lucky had trouble with long sentences. And he was starting to become nervous. Something about this customer made him uncomfortable, and he needed a cigarette. Even five minutes without a smoke left him agitated. It had been more than five minutes.

"What are you giving me for the coasters?" Mortimer asked.

"One dollar," Lucky whistled.

"Those are original *Star Trek* coasters."

Lucky nodded.

"Not *Next Generation* or *Deep Space Nine.*"

"One dollar."

Mortimer felt outraged. The coasters were a collector's item. They would bring at least six or seven dollars on the open market. He ran through the calculations in his mind. Even allowing for carrying costs, the pawn broker would still make a return of five or six hundred percent—not as good as the return on papaya drink, but better than he liked to have earned at his expense.

Mortimer Taylor Coleridge could not be had. He was going to give Lucky a piece of mind.

Then it struck him.

He had no need for any of it now. He did not need the semi-soft twin mattress or the twelve-inch black and white television. He did not need the Cuisinart or the counter-top grilling machine endorsed by the former professional boxer. He did not need the *Star Trek* coasters. He would not be having any more cocktail parties. He did not even need the few extra bucks he might haggle out of the emphysemic store owner. He made more than he needed at the Papaya Queen.

What he needed was to be free.

So he sold it, his life, for three hundred dollars.

When he returned to his flat on 185th Street and Broadway, he looked over all that he had kept: a small compact disk player, his No Doubt disks, and two books: Walt Whitman's *Leaves of Grass* and *Siddartha* by Herman Hesse. The entirety of his worldly possessions now fit upon the sill of the lone window of his studio. The window looked out into an elevator shaftway. The elevator had not run in decades.

From that day on Mortimer lived an ascetic life.

He woke early in the mornings, long before the sun rose over the sleepy island of Manhattan. He did not need an alarm buzzer to wake him; his energy came from within now. He slept on the floor, sitting up, a practice he believed to be an important step in his mastery over himself, and he allowed himself to sleep for no more than four hours. Despite these changes, Mortimer felt more rested in the mornings than he ever did in the days when he would lounge in his bed, pressing the snooze button numerous times, never feeling quite ready to meet the world. Now he could hardly wait to begin each new day.

He began by tending to his body. He started with push-ups and sit-ups, two hundred to start. Over time the number grew. In a few weeks he could complete a thousand of each without becoming winded. His biceps swelled; his stomach grew taut and rippled.

After that he spent an hour practicing the honored Chinese art of Tai-Chi, a series of practiced gestures that developed efficiency of movement and helped to quiet the spirit through controlled breathing. Mortimer studied at the hands of a master, Wan G. Jew, the owner of the Chinese laundry on the corner of St. Nicholas Avenue and 184th Street. At 5:00 each morning Mortimer walked down to Imperial Cleaners. There, in front of the store, the guru guided his disciple through the sacred movements, imparting upon Mortimer all of his abundant collected wisdom.

Wan G. Jew was glad for the company. During the forty years he had lived in the United States, he had always performed his morning exercises alone. He was generally uncomfortable with people. The smell of percethylene had bonded permanently to his hands, which made him reticent and self-conscious. But the strange looking young man did not seem to mind and for this Wan G. Jew gave thanks. In fact the smell, which faintly resembled Papaya, invigorated Mortimer. Mortimer loved the study of the ancient art. He left the sessions feeling energized and buoyant.

After that he ran four miles, ritualistically the same route each day: out through Inwood Park, a forgotten treasure of trees and cobblestone paths hidden away in the northwest corner of the city, then back along the Hudson River, past the homeless men and the feral dogs that hid in the weeds along the riverbank. Sometimes the dogs chased him, but Mortimer had grown quick and agile, and they could not stay with him for long.

The homeless men showed no interest in him at all.

After his run he practiced Yoga. He had no experience in the art; he learned entirely through mimicry. At first he used rudimentary guides from a tablemat he saved from a vegetarian Chinese restaurant, and some positions that he had seen Sting contort himself into in the *Behind the Music* telling the remarkable story of the singer's own life. Later he purchased basic texts from vendors who lined the streets of Broadway on Sunday mornings.

These were old books, paperbacks with worn-out covers whose titles were often not visible. This did not concern Mortimer. The practice of Yoga had not changed in thousands of years. And the books only cost fifty cents, which sometimes could be bargained down to a quarter. Mortimer did not see how there could be much profit in this, even if the vendor acquired the books for free, but this was not his concern.

He learned the Yoga poses: *ustrasana*, the camel, *setu bandha sarvangasana*, the bridge, *mudhasana*, the pose of the child. He learned the mantras: *Om*, the sound of all life, the sound of the universe. In time he began to feel *prana*, the energy of the universe flowing through his body. The practice made him strong and flexible; power surged through his veins.

In all he spent five hours each morning on his exercises, a demanding program that he knew would be beyond most people. Sometimes he doubted whether even he could withstand the pain. But the exertions offered their own rewards. Mortimer felt lithe and supple when he finished, fully charged to meet the day. And even were this not the case, he nevertheless would have put himself through these same paces. Physical training was a critical component of his preparations. She would be drawn to him for his mind not his body, as he was drawn to her own mind, but his body would be the first thing that she would see. Mortimer understood that how one treated their body spoke volumes about his image of himself and his approach to life. She would understand this too.

The statement his body made about himself had once been

confused and ambiguous. Now it spoke loud and clear: this man was at peace with the world and with himself. Even through the "Snappy Service" smock that she would first see him in, she would not be able to help but see his glow. This would draw her to him.

He purged his body, starving himself sometimes for days at a time. This cleansed him, rinsing his body of the toxins of urban life. More importantly, it helped to teach him patience. If he could wait for food, despite his body's yearnings, he could wait for anything. This was a skill he also would need. She could come at any time—it could be days or years, there was no way to tell and there would be little warning. He could not afford impetuousness. So he taught himself to wait.

When he did eat, he ate in moderation. He made sure to always leave a little room in his stomach. He ate pure foods such as fruits and vegetables, nuts and seeds, cheeses, and, of course, the occasional Papaya Queen frankfurter, the purest food of all.

In the evenings he tended to his mind. He sat on the floor in the bound lotus pose and relaxed his mind, silencing his thoughts. With practice he became aware only of his body and his breathing, then not even that. His senses grew acute. He became more aware of himself and his surroundings. The benefits of meditation extended to his day-to-day life. He grew more mindful of his surroundings, more prepared to meet the challenges of life. In the language of Yoga, he dispensed of *avidya*, incorrect comprehension, and attained *vidya*, correct understanding. His mind became as supple as his body. This was as important as his physical state of being. His heightened awareness would make him more sensitive to the situation when she arrived. He would be better able to respond to her cues, more nimble in dealing with things however they transpired.

He passed day after day in this manner. His mind grew quiet. He began to hear his internal voice. It urged patience. So in his tiny room with the window that looked out upon the non-functioning elevator, Mortimer Taylor Coleridge kneeled upon the floor, crossed his legs, opened his palms to the sky, and touched his forefingers to the thumbs, the *mudra* of the Om.

And sat.

And waited.

20.

From the journal of Mortimer Taylor Coleridge

Thaddeus Johnson and I met on Tuesday afternoons, in his dreary office in the corner of the eighth floor of the Ward's Island Psychiatric Center, a spot upon which the world had turned its back. Everything about the space made clear that life had no place there. The paint, a drab industrial pink to begin with, had faded over the years. Dr. Johnson had spare decorations—a few diplomas, professional journals, an award or two from some community organization or another. Only one adornment had any color: a needlepoint pillow propped in the corner of his couch. It looked quite old, and the yarn had faded over time. It said:

"World's Greatest Dad"

The office had a view of the Triboro Bridge. An inch of dust covered the window, yet enough light still came through that it might have given the office some vibrancy and connected it to the rest of the world, but Thaddeus Johnson always kept the tattered red shades drawn. He did this out of habit, I imagine, a practice developed to help him focus better on his patients.

The usefulness of this practice had been outlived since Thaddeus Johnson was senile. He wasn't quite getting–lost–in–the–park–without–being–able–to–remember–where–you–live senile, but remembering anything from one week to another was out of the question. And Dr. Johnson was not very accomplished at compensating for his increasing limitations. He took spare notes, which meant that each session recapitulated all of the others. Johnson should have been fired, or ushered into retirement with a rubber chicken dinner, but the protections of civil service made this impractical.

"Spell it out for me, Mortimer" he said one Tuesday, or every Tuesday. "Spell out your belief that humans are worms."

Most of our sessions went something like this. My folder contained a notation, which said:

LUNATIC–BELIEVES HUMANS ARE WORMS

which Johnson would review each time before seeing me, then ask me this same question, with great sincerity as if he were asking it for the first time, even though we had been over the same ground dozens of times before. This would send us down a path that would include an extensive discussion of my family, followed by Dr. Johnson's belief that this family history contributed to my belief system, and finally to my own skepticism about the value of therapy. Each time it went a little differently, but not by very much. It had all been programmed, like a bad television rerun—*Gomer Pyle* or *McHale's Navy*—played over and over.

I shook my head, frustrated. "I don't believe that humans are worms," I said. "I believe that humans exhibit many types of the same behavior as worms and that all of the differences that we think make us superior really aren't differences at all."

"Like agriculture," he said.

He had a way of doing this, of summarizing a position in a

manner that made it seem patently absurd. It would be a waste of time to try to correct him, however, because within an hour, he would forget what he had said.

"Right," I said. "Like agriculture."

"And art."

"And art."

"The New Guinean bowerbirds."

He had jotted down some sort of note to himself about the bowerbirds. They always came up.

I sighed. "Yes. The New Guinean bowerbirds."

"And the consequence of this is what?"

"Could it be more obvious?"

I watched hopefully for a sign of understanding. We had been over this so many times before; each session was a maddening repeat of an already-played chess game. He made his moves, I made mine, over and over. This time, I hoped, we would break the cycle. I watched his face, watched for a sign of understanding. None came. He just sat and waited for me to say more.

I sighed again.

"We don't think animals have free will, right? We don't think that when ants build an anthill or when salmon swim upstream that they are exercising choice. When a dog bites the ear off of a little child, we don't put it on trial for assault. We don't believe it is acting maliciously because we don't believe that it is capable of rational choice. It just does what it is genetically programmed to do. It's just acting on instinct. Right?"

Johnson said nothing.

"Before we can believe that humans have free will, we need to find something that makes humans different from animals. There has to be evidence of some type of behavior that we engage in that they don't. But there isn't. Everything we do, they do. Everything they do, we do. We eat when we're hungry, we sleep when we're tired. We have sex with people whom we find attractive for reasons we can't begin to articulate. We try to lure mates by painting beautiful pictures and by driving fancy cars.

"With almost everything we do, we can't say why we do it. We have a favorite color, we don't know why. We like rainbows, we don't know why. Music, art, ice cream, it's all the same. We don't choose our taste for these things; they choose us. We do things we know we shouldn't. We lie. We cheat. We fall in love in spite of ourselves. We do all of these things against our best judgment, and yet we insist on continuing this myth that somehow we are in control.

"We don't have free will. Animals don't have it. And we're just animals."

"And this is what Professor Skinny said?"

"No," I said. "No, he didn't say this. We've been over this before. He said everything except this. But it's the extension of it. It's the only conclusion that follows logically from what he said. If you demonstrate that all of the things that make us distinctively human are determined by genetics and that they have behavioral analogues in ordinary animals, what other conclusion could one reach? He just didn't want to say it. He wanted us to reach the conclusion for ourselves."

"What about emotions?" asked Johnson. "What about our conscience? Humans have a sense of right and wrong. Animals don't, do they?"

"What does that mean to have a sense of right and wrong? Animals learn that certain types of berries give them stomachaches just like babies learn that hot things burn. Maybe man is a little more sophisticated at it. Man can calculate what is in his long-term interest. He might decline to eat a pile of sugar, even though it's a source of quick energy, because he knows it will make him feel sick and make him fat. But he's not really doing anything different than animals do."

Johnson started to speak, but I anticipated his response.

"I know what you're thinking," I said. I knew, of course, because he had offered the same answer dozens of times before, though he had no recollection of this. "You're asking yourself, 'what about things that people do that aren't in their interest, such as altruistic behavior, moral behavior?' But this isn't any different than what animals do. Birds that care for their young put themselves at risk. That's altruistic behavior. They're invested with an instinct to care for their children. It's no different with us. How many times have you heard a father say that his life changed the moment that he saw his son or daughter? When the offspring arrive, their bodies are flooded with hormones. They are thereby being programmed to care for their children.

"We may put fancy names on it. We might say we're doing something because it's utilitarian or satisfies some other philosophical principle. But this is all just a rationalization. Our programming tells us what philosophy to find appealing. We just do what our instincts tell us to do.

"Tell me," I said. "How often have you ever done something that you felt was wrong in your gut? How often have you convinced yourself to behave in a certain way because some philosophical principle told you that it was the right thing to do?"

Johnson nodded but said nothing. Johnson had forgotten many things. He may even have forgotten his children's names. But he had not forgotten his basic training to never, ever answer a patient's question.

"What about love?" he asked. "Animals can't love, can they?"

I was ready for this, of course.

"The question isn't whether animals are capable of love," I said. "The question is whether humans are. Animals can bond to a mate for life. Swans do, other types of birds too. Most are far more faithful to their spouses than humans are. Does this mean they love? Does this mean they have made a calculated choice that their mate is the one with whom they want to spend eternity? Or is it just another surge of hormones that makes them feel things they cannot explain?

"Is it any different with people? A human being doesn't sit in his room and dispassionately construct his ideal type and then go forth into the world and find someone to match that description. He goes to work and lives his life and all of sudden discovers one day that he has fallen in love, for reasons that he does not understand. Maybe then he rationalizes things, emphasizes the qualities of his lover that match what his mind tells him is good for him, and de-emphasizes the ones that don't jibe. He tries to fit the person into the schema. But that's the mind working to perpetuate the myth of volition. The man doesn't control the feelings. The feelings control the man.

"We're no different than animals in this regard, doctor. We serve an unseen master."

"The nucleic acids."

"Yes, the nucleic acids."

"Which is why love is not possible."

"Love is not possible—at least not in any sense that would make it of interest to anyone."

"And this is something else that Dr. Skinny believed."

"No, he left this question unresolved."

"But this is the conclusion that you chose to reach."

"It is the only conclusion that follows from his teachings."

"And this led to your belief that life was without point."

"Simplified perhaps, but essentially true."

"And this is why you did what you did?"

"Yes."

"Out of despair?"

"Out of rationality."

21.

It seems important to interrupt at this point to explicate the circumstances that led to Thaddeus Johnson taking Mortimer under his care and the event to which the doctor refers at the end of the preceding excerpt from Mortimer's diary.

At the conclusion of the spring 1990 semester, most of the students in Biology 235 returned to their lives without giving a second thought to the course or to the rather unorthodox teachings of their professor. This included the few students who weathered the entire lecture series. This also included Dr. Skinny himself, who on the last day of class had his bags packed in his office and a car waiting for him outside the faculty building. The limousine whisked him to Newark Airport, from which he flew non-stop to the island of Puerto Rico, where he had an apartment on the beach and a pretty, young girlfriend. She made Skinny forget about evolutionary biology and most everything else.

Back home the students waited patiently for their As and A-minuses, which they received in due course. Everyone's lives returned to normal—everyone, that is, except Mortimer Taylor Coleridge. He received a B-plus, the lowest grade in the class. The mark was not intended to censure Mortimer; it did not reflect upon the quality of his work or his level of preparation. It could be attributed entirely to his poor penmanship. Mortimer wrote copiously on the subject of the exam, filling more than seven blue books with his ruminations about the meaning of life. But the unfortunate graduate student grading the exams could read none of it. He tried for hours to decipher the handwriting, without success; it appeared to him to be nothing more than a massive scribble. In a quandary, the teaching fellow settled on the grade of B-plus, which compromised between his expectation that some of what the 112 pages of exposition contained must be coherent and responsive, and his own belief—despite Professor Skinny's clear instruction to be exceedingly lenient—that he should not award a grade of A without having been able to make out at least one word of what the student had written.

The B plus, though, is not the reason that Mortimer's life failed to return to normal.

It went much deeper than that.

Professor Skinny's teachings haunted Mortimer. He thought about them day and night. While other students passed the summer working in camps and fast food stores and drinking beer and chasing girls, while Professor Skinny himself spent the days basking in the Caribbean sun and the evenings making love to the nineteen year-old daughter of his housekeeper, while life went on all around him, Mortimer sat from dawn to dusk in his favorite place, the window table at the Papaya Queen on the corner of 110th and Amsterdam, and read everything he could find on the subject of evolutionary biology. He filled one notebook after another with his thoughts—he always kept a notebook with him—and turned the subject over and over in his mind.

He could find no flaw in Skinny's proof. It was infallible. No one could deny this. Mortimer searched far and wide for examples of human behavior that the professor had not considered. He came up with a few: war, altruism, plumbing. All had analogues in the animal kingdom. All had genetic precursors. All, in other words, had been programmed.

But the proof of the impossibility of free choice was only part of the issue. It did not gratify Mortimer. It did not send him dancing into the streets in glee, but it also did not send him into despair. He could stand the thought of being nothing more than an automaton. He could imagine worse fates than this. Something else that followed from Skinny's argument bothered him more. It was again not something that the professor had said, but again too no other conclusion could follow. It was this corollary that sent him spiraling downward: Mortimer recognized that individual choices did not matter.

This was the genius of evolution, the essence of diversity. What ensured the survival of the nucleic acids was that no single event or individual could foil them. Each time one of their conduits met some stress or crisis, some would respond in one way, others another. Some would die, but the survival of the group would be assured. The alternative, allowing the machines freedom to act, carried with it the risk that everyone would make the same choice and that that choice would prove to be the wrong one. So the acids did not allow for it. They hedged their bets. Whatever situation arose, for whatever species, some would choose one path, some another.

This sent Mortimer reeling. He could tolerate being insignificant. He could stand the thought of being nothing more than a chess piece manipulated by an unseen hand. He could even tolerate being a trivial pawn in that game. He could stand all of this, so long as the game in which he participated had importance. But Professor Skinny had showed that it was not important. Every day, every conceivable board was being played out in every conceivable way. Nature didn't even need to try in any of the games; it just played out all of the infinite permutations, moving one way in one game and another in the other. So it was bound to win at least a few.

Nothing mattered. No decision had significance. If one species of fish laid its eggs under rocks, another would bury them in the soil. If some worms burrowed down in the rain, others waded to the surface. If some aardvarks ate salty foods, others spit them out. Every imaginable decision, whether insignificant or grave, made no difference, since someone else would be instructed to choose the opposite.

Whether to have many spouses or one.

Whether to turn left at the road or right.

Whether to live or to die.

None of it mattered. Or at least so Mortimer believed.

So one day, confident that the act would be of no consequence, Mortimer decided to end his life. It would be of no consequence because somewhere else in the world, someone in his circumstances, confronted with the same information and same life situation, would choose the opposite course of action. The acids would see to this.

Mortimer thought it did not even make sense to think of this act as a choice. He had been programmed with a mix of chemicals and electrical charges that led him to view death as the rational course of action given the arguably depressing circumstances that then confronted him. He was merely carrying out the program.

Mortimer did not give much thought to the method by which he would achieve his demise. One July afternoon he treated himself to a double helping of Papaya Queen, then walked home to his dormitory room, where he went to the bathroom and opened the medicine cabinet. There he found a nearly full bottle of aspirin. He swallowed the entire contents, thirty-seven tablets in all, sat down on the tattered recliner in the common area, and waited.

As it turned out, though, the bottle did not contain aspirin. The putative analgesic belonged to one of Mortimer's summer roommates, Harold Munch, from Chevy Chase, Maryland, a gangly and sickly looking boy with toothpick arms and bulging eyes, swollen from years of staring at computer screens and Dungeons & Dragons monster manuals. Munch suffered from chronic headaches, so he kept an ample supply of aspirin at the ready. From the beginning of the summer, tension in the room had persisted between Munch and the third member of their rooming group, Billy Matson from Madison, Wisconsin, a fine football player and nice enough fellow, but not the keenest of wits.

Both Munch and Matson tolerated Mortimer well enough. He struck them both as incomprehensibly strange, and since they didn't know what to make of him, they avoided him. Mortimer obliged by spending most of his time out of the room, usually at the Papaya Queen, where he liked to watch the crowds and read. But Matson hated Munch, whom he found weak and pathetic, from the first day. And Munch in turn hated Matson, whom he regarded as the beneficiary of the perverse brand of affirmative action practiced in the Ivy League, affirmative action that benefits those born with the combination of genes that gave them a surfeit of muscle, but not much in the way of smarts. In the case of Columbia University it seemed particularly perverse since the accommodation had failed to produce much in the way of victory on the gridiron.

It was bad luck really that the roommates ended up together in the summer economics class, sitting next to each other because of the proximity of their names in the alphabet. They were taking the class for opposite reasons: Munch to get a leg up on his junior year, Matson because he had failed it in the spring. The day before Mortimer's attempted overdose, Munch earned the special enmity of Matson by refusing to clandestinely assist his roommate with one of the questions on their midterm examination.

Matson leaned forward and whispered, "Harold, who heads the World Bank?"

Munch tilted his head ever so slightly, so the proctor would not notice. "The Elders of Zion," he whispered back.

This was not the correct answer, of course. The anti-Semitic reference earned Billy Matson a talking-to from the professor and a reprimand from the dean, which included a one game suspension for the fall season, when Matson had been slated to start at quarterback. Matson had never even heard of the Elders of Zion, but he could not very well defend himself by saying that the answer had been given to him by a classmate mischievously trying to thwart his cheating. So he apologized and accepted the punishment, but not without uttering a silent vow of revenge, which he achieved the next day by replacing Harold Munch's aspirin with stool softener.

So the consumption of the pills did not lead to Mortimer's death, only to a severe case of diarrhea, and to a stay at the Ward's Island Psychiatric Center, a good hospital, and to his being taken under the care of Thaddeus Johnson in the early stages of his senility, not the best doctor perhaps, but by all accounts a fine father.

22.

From the journal of Mortimer Taylor Coleridge

I knew what would come next. We had repeated this pattern many times before, too. Johnson would try for a while to poke some hole in my reasoning until he exhausted himself—he had no hope of finding any such flaw—at which point he would retreat from my territory to his, turning to more traditional therapeutic methodologies.

"Tell me again about your parents." Johnson rolled a pen between his thumb and fingers, an objectionable habit that became insufferable when he asked a question he had asked a hundred times before, as he had this one, as he had all of them. But pointing this out to him would accomplish nothing; it would lead only to acrimonious questioning about why I felt it necessary to challenge his methods or why the rolling of the pen disturbed me. The sessions went smoother if I answered without protest.

"My mother died when I was three," I said. "From Scarlet Fever." I knew what Johnson would say before he said it, of course; he said the same thing every time.

"I thought they had eradicated Scarlet Fever."

"No, there are still a few cases," I said amiably. "It's scarlet letters that they've done away with."

Johnson nodded.

"I have only one memory of her. I was lying in my crib. It was late in the evening. I couldn't have been more than one or two. She was reading poetry to me. I don't remember what it was, of course. I just remember the sound of her voice, soothing me. She loved poetry. Before she gave birth to me she taught English in a junior high school.

"Anyway, she died, leaving my father to take care of me, which was not something he was equipped to do. He was a marginal, itinerant physicist who made his living going from college to college picking up the odd teaching job. He never stayed in any one place for long. This was fine when my mother was alive. Sometimes she followed him around, picking up work herself. After I was born, though, she settled in New York. He would come home for holidays and semester breaks.

"After she died, he took me with him on a few of his jaunts. I remember going with him to Indiana or Iowa, or someplace like that. I know it began with an "I." But having me along became a hardship for him, and after a while he started leaving me at home with my maternal grandparents. He would still come home for holidays and semester breaks. But then he started picking up teaching work in the summer. And then he started missing Thanksgivings, and a Christmas or two. He would call and say how sorry he was, that he had too much work to do, too many papers to grade. Then he stopped calling. He got married again and had a new family, in Idaho I think. I overheard my grandparents talking about it one day. They didn't realize that I heard.

"So my grandparents raised me, which was fine. They were nice people and they tried their best, but they were old, well into their eighties at the end. The last couple of years I took care of them as much as they took care of me. They died when I was fifteen, one after the other in the span of six weeks. After my grandmother died, my grandfather had no reason to live. It was as if he willed himself to die. It was sweet, really, in a way. Anyway, they left me just enough money so that I could take care of myself through high school. Then Columbia gave me a scholarship. You know the rest."

The history became shorter each time I delivered it, a novel edited down to a short story, then to an even shorter essay. An entire life reduced to four paragraphs.

Thaddeus Johnson carefully thought over what I had said. To his credit he did so every time, the careful, contemplative deliberation of a well-meaning man. He would mull it all over, rolling the pen between his thumb and forefinger. Then the light bulb would come on over his head. This felt strange, to see a man having the same epiphanies over and over.

"I have a thought," he said.

Showing interest, I widened my eyes.

"It seems to me that your family background helps explain your willingness to credit the rather eccentric ideas of your professor. The fact of your father walking out on you is very painful to you, more painful than you care to admit to yourself. One way of coping with that pain would be to believe that your father did not have a choice in his actions. Better to think that he had to do it than to believe that he simply chose to reject you. So this Professor Skinny's fanciful notion that humans lack free will, that we are nothing more than hormone-driven robots, has great appeal to you. It makes sense. It explains why you've jumped into this whole thing without thinking.

"It has nothing to do with the ideas themselves; it's what the ideas do for your self-image. You could just as easily believe that aliens abducted your father or that he wasn't your father at all. It would all accomplish the same thing. It's just a choice. You've chosen to believe this. You could also choose to believe that your father is a human being and that he made a mistake and forgive him for his acts. This would be a healthier choice, certainly a lot less debilitating than this self-deception that life doesn't matter."

Then I would say something like, "That's what's wrong with your entire approach. You look only at the motivations behind the things people say. You don't examine at all the validity of what they are saying.

"I mean who is deceiving whom? You call Professor Skinny's ideas fanciful, but you haven't come up with a single logical argument to refute them. You consider the existence of free will as a proven fact, even though no evidence exists to support it. Whose motivations should be in question?

"You want to talk about logical explanations. Which is more likely, that free will exists or that the belief in free will evolved as a coping mechanism? Human beings seem to be unique in one respect: they evolved intelligence sophisticated enough to understand the forces that led to their creation. Once they did, wouldn't they also have to evolve a belief in free will? Could they live otherwise? Could they live understanding that they were just sophisticated machines, whose job it was to eat and have sex, with no control over what they liked to eat and who they wanted to screw?

"Doesn't this help explain why human beings are so willing to take things on faith? Doesn't it explain religion? How else do you account for humans' willingness to worship gods that they have never seen, to believe in an afterlife unsupported by any evidence, to fear retribution from an unproven source?' They are more willing to adhere to a code of conduct from an unseen god than they are to take action because they reason it to be moral.

"Isn't it because it has to be this way? They have to believe that there is an order to life. They have to believe that things happen for a reason, that some omniscient entity sees everything they do with rewards and punishments to be doled out later. They have to believe that choices matter. The alternative would be massive despair. The species would not endure. This must have been the way we evolved. Our very existence proves that it happened.

"Doesn't this make the most sense? Deep down people know they are programmed. They know that they cannot escape who they are. They keep repeating the same things over and over, the same choices, the same mistakes, and yet they go on living because of this delusion of control, this myth that it all means something.

"Who is deceiving whom?"

But this never satisfied Johnson. He would think about my words for a while, always with the same solemn sincerity. Then, inevitably he would say the same thing:

"Happiness is a choice. Everything is a choice."

We would then fight back and forth, repeating the same arguments over and over, Johnson with greater vigor, since from his perspective he had never had the argument before. Then the hourglass on his desk would bring the fifty-minute hour to a close, and he would say that we would pick it up the next time, which meant that we would start over again at the beginning, and Johnson would scratch a note on the folder that there had been no progress or something to that effect.

And so it went.

Week after week, the same arguments replayed over and over. Finally, one week it just seemed easier to give the answer that I knew he wanted to hear. So when he made his speech about happiness being a choice, I said, "You know, we have talked about this many times before and I am starting now to see your point. You have been very persuasive. Lots of different conclusions could be drawn from the evidence. That I chose the most depressing one says more, I think, about me than it does about any philosophical position. Today I choose to be happy. I choose to live."

Dr. Johnson smiled and made a note on the folder. "Great progress today," it said.

After a few weeks of reiterating my conviction that therapy had shown me the light, Dr. Johnson said one Tuesday, "You have made great progress, Mortimer. It's time for you to go home." He didn't remember anything about my progress, of course. It was simply that I had accumulated enough positive notations on the folder to merit dismissal.

So I went home.

And when I did, I found that my decision had built up some momentum behind it. Saying the words "I choose to live" so many times gave them the force of inertia. Whether I lived or died made no difference, of course; these were merely different courses, no one would care which I followed. Whatever I chose, someone else would choose differently. By then it just seemed easier to go on living. So I took a job doing something that felt comfortable and familiar and I rented an apartment. I bought things: a television, talcum powder, an electric knife. I found a girlfriend who sometimes helped make the emptiness more bearable, but mostly didn't. I went on living. Not by act of will, or conviction, just by default.

And so it went.

Until I met her.

23.

In the evenings, after he finished his meditations and study, Mortimer would wander the streets for hours, aimlessly, watching people eat pizza in pizza parlors, or race from one place to another, or stagger into taxicabs on their way home from the bars. His existence had grown so solitary that he craved human contact of any kind.

One night, he happened upon an Internet cafe, not far from Papaya Queen. Here he discovered a new world he had missed on his previous research expeditions, dozens of chat rooms devoted to Gwen Stefani, where people would discuss every detail of her life: what she wore, whom she was dating, where she had been seen. Most of the people were favorably disposed to her. She had a loyal following that cut across all social divisions. But some had mischief on their mind. They criticized her clothes and her music and spread baseless rumors about her personal life.

Mortimer took up her causes. When someone posted a message that they had seen footage of her in a pornographic movie, Mortimer called the person into a private chat room where he explained that he represented Gwen Stefani and that the person would find a libel lawsuit tacked to his front door in the morning if he did not recant the message within thirty minutes. It took ten.

When *steflove24* criticized Gwen's hair, Mortimer scoured the Internet for a picture of the woman. He found it at a website for overweight singles. The woman weighed three hundred pounds and her hair had split ends. Mortimer posted the picture. Disgraced, she disappeared from the chat room forever.

No offense was too small. Anyone criticizing the lyrics from a No Doubt song found his own grammar dissected. Any criticism of Gwen's physical appearance was disposed of in the same manner as *steflove24*. The naysayers grew timid. Dissent was stifled.

With time, Mortimer grew bolder, taking up grudges that he thought Gwen would have or should have held. He crusaded online against the singer Moby, who practiced a mindless brand of techno-pop, which Mortimer disdained.

Gwen sang a duet with Moby on a song called "Southside," on the CD *Play*. The two-voiced version of "Southside" became popular on radio stations, but Moby did not see fit to include it on the album, instead using a solo recording, which Mortimer understood to send the clear message that Moby regarded Gwen as someone to be exploited for commercial gain, but who did not meet the one-named singer's exacting standards for true art.

So Mortimer slandered him. He posted messages that he had seen Moby, an avowed vegan, in McDonald's and shopping for shoes at Kenneth Cole. He reported that the singer had been observed dining at a posh restaurant with executives from Exxon, courting an endorsement deal, and other tidbits that undermined

Moby's carefully maintained image of environmental sensitivity. Slowly but surely, Moby's sales dropped. It was satisfyingly ironic to Mortimer that later, after Gwen's star had eclipsed his own, Moby re-released the CD with the duet version of "Southside."

Mortimer perceived a role for himself as Gwen's advocate. He relished the day when he could share with her his successes on her behalf. She would embrace the idea of his fulfilling this function, he knew. To prepare for it, Mortimer performed other favors for her. He took the initiative of correcting the grammar in her songs. He rectified the punctuation mistake in the lyrics to the hit song "Ex-Girlfriend" from *Return to Saturn*, removing the superfluous comma between "ex-girl" and "friend" in the chorus. He corrected the mistaken use of the singular in "Doormat," from the band's first album. "Well, there's more fish in the sea" became "Well, there are more fish in the sea." And he corrected the most egregious error of all, in the band's breakthrough hit "Don't Speak," about Gwen's breakup with Tony. It began:

You and me
We used to be together
Every day together always

thus confusing the nominative and subjective cases. It should properly have begun "you and I." Mortimer thought to simply correct the error, but he recognized that this would undermine the assonance between "me" and "we" and "be" in the second line, so he undertook to rewrite the entire stanza, settling ultimately upon this revision:

You and I

Erstwhile sidekicks,
Our ties bind tight, as thieves we are thick

Mortimer grew to prefer this formulation. He envisioned that the band would re-release the song, or perhaps even the entire album, with this headline emblazoned across the cover:

GRAMMATICALLY CORRECT VERSION

This would please her even more, he knew. But what would please her most of all would be that she finally had an intellectual partner in her endeavors, someone who shared her philosophy and message and who possessed the substance to correct her occasional mistakes. This would please her very much, indeed.

24.

From the journal of Mortimer Taylor Coleridge

For these many months that I have been preparing myself, I have thought about what I will say to her when we meet. The prospect of this occupies my every waking hour since what I say could not be more important. I shall have only one chance to make a first impression and scarce time to impress myself upon her. The words will need to grab her attention quickly, and establish my credibility. She will know from looking at me that I am not an ordinary hot dog vendor, but only words can suggest to her the sacrifices that I have made and the special bond that exists between us. I will have no margin for error.

Siddartha has come to mind, of course. The poem that Siddartha creates upon meeting Kamala seems perfect. It is too long, but perhaps an excerpt would do:

> *As he saw the lotus flower,*
> *Deeply he bowed.*

But will she know Hesse? If she does not, she will love it when I introduce it to her, but this will be of little consolation if there is no second meeting. The reference must be accessible, significant without context. Perhaps Keats instead:

> *Beauty is truth, truth beauty—that is all*
> *Ye know on earth, and all ye need to know*

Even if she does not know the poem, the words will have impact. But I fear this too romantic. It could overwhelm her, scare her away. The point is not to impress my love upon her. That will come in time. The sole object is to make her take notice, to let her see that the man standing before her is self-aware, like she, a member of the most elite of all fraternities. Whitman would do well:

I believe in you my soul, the other I am must not abase itself to you
And you must not be abased to the other.

But again, what if she has not read it? And so it has gone for months on end, over and over. Different words for consideration, Dickinson, Shakespeare, Kant, all well suited for the task, but all riddled with the uncertainty of accessibility.

And then all at once it comes to me. Again it should have been obvious. Again the answer has been before me all the while. Once more her own words held the answer, her own ruminations from "Different People," about the diversity of life:

Look at me, I'm a person
Look at me, I'm my own person

These are the words I will use.

25.

While wandering the streets one evening, Mortimer passed Skyscraper Records, where to his surprise he found Violet Blayer and Bertrand Fuddle standing outside the store, immersed in a heated conversation. Even from across the street, Mortimer could see that Fuddle was riddled with oxytocin. His eyes bulged and his shoulders hunched over in supplication as he held a bushel of flowers in his hand. He scarcely resembled the man Mortimer knew from the store. Violet, though, looked much as Mortimer remembered.

Neither Violet nor Fuddle noticed Mortimer approaching from the other side of the avenue, and Mortimer decided to take advantage of the opportunity. He walked around the entire block, out of sight, approaching them this time from the other side of the store. Because the couple stood near the corner, Mortimer was able, by positioning himself near the adjacent edge of the store, to witness their conversation without being noticed.

It became clear to Mortimer in short order that Violet and Fuddle had been dating each other for some time, perhaps even since that day, months ago, when Fuddle had wrapped his cloak around her. Mortimer chided himself for having failed to notice this. He felt shamefully unobservant. But he had no other reaction one way or the other. He certainly felt no pangs of jealousy or regret. Mortimer just listened. Fuddle and Violet were discussing plans of some sort.

"I told you," she said. "I can't go out with you this weekend."

"I don't understand why not."

"I'm going to visit my mother. We've been through this before."

"But you went to see your mother last weekend. And the weekend before that."

"She is a very important person in my life."

"And I'm not?"

Violet frowned. Mortimer could see her face through the window of the store. He had a perfect vantage point, over the shoulder of a life-sized cutout of Barbra Streisand, which preserved his anonymity. Mortimer recognized Violet's frown; he had seen it many times before.

"Of course you're an important person to me," she said.

"But not as important as your mother."

"I didn't say that."

Fuddle took off his glasses and rubbed his frog eyes. Calmer, he said, "It just seems to me that if you loved me you would want to spend more time with me. We haven't been together in two months."

Violet pursed her lips. She did this when she felt uncomfortable.

"I told you, Bert. I love you, but I'm not in love with you."

"What does that mean?"

"It means I don't want to date you. We can be good friends, but that's all."

Fuddle looked down at the floor, hurt.

"Bert, we've been through this several times before. It's the same thing, over and over. Why can't you hear what I'm saying?"

Fuddle stared at the ground as he spoke. "You told me I was perfect. You told me I was kinder to you than anyone you had ever been with."

She smiled. "You were."

"You said I treated you better, that I thought about your needs more, listened more carefully to what you had to say."

"You did. You do."

"Then why don't you love me?"

She looked down now. "I don't know," she said.

They stayed that way for a while, each looking at the ground, neither speaking. Finally Bertrand Fuddle raised his head and asked, quite sheepishly, "It's because you still love him, isn't it?"

Violet said nothing. She just stared at Fuddle for a while, a hint of exasperation on her face. Mortimer knew this look too. Finally she said, "I have to go back to work." And she walked into the store, without looking back, leaving Fuddle on the street corner by himself.

Fuddle stayed there for a while as Mortimer watched

him through the glass. He seemed lost, completely lost, like someone who does not know where they have been or where they are going or even where they are. He turned around in place, unable to decide upon a direction or a course of action. He still held the flowers in his hand. They had started to droop, which made him all the more pathetic. Finally, he dropped them in the wastebasket, fixed his polyester tie and sport coat, and walked into the record store.

Mortimer waited a few minutes and then followed him in. He could not resist.

He found Fuddle in the pop section, looking over albums by an artist named Madonna, who wrote songs about Jewish mysticism and virginity and overprotective parents. Mortimer thought well of Madonna, but she could not compare with Gwen. She did not write and sing with the same openness and honesty. No one did. Mortimer picked out a No Doubt CD, *Tragic Kingdom*, and walked over to Fuddle with the idea of recommending it to him.

"Hello, Mr. Fuddle," he said.

Fuddle was taken aback; he had not anticipated running into anyone he knew, least of all Mortimer Coleridge. He took a moment to compose himself, and when he answered, it was in the formal manner Mortimer had grown accustomed to at work.

"Hello, Mortimer," he said.

"What brings you out tonight?"

"Just some shopping."

Mortimer nodded at the disc in Fuddle's hand.

"A Madonna fan?" he asked.

"Yes."

"What's your favorite album?"

Fuddle didn't answer. Throughout the short conversation he had been staring past Mortimer on and off, distracted by something in the distance. Now he could not take his eyes from it. Mortimer turned ever so slightly; he did not want Fuddle to notice him looking. Out of the corner of his eye, Mortiner saw Violet running out of the store, tears in her eyes. Mortimer turned back quickly, so that when Fuddle regained his composure he concluded that Mortimer had noticed nothing.

"I'm sorry," Fuddle said. "I forgot what you said."

"I was asking about your favorite album."

Fuddle nodded, but he soon became distracted again. He stared out the front window of the store, his eyes tracing a line from left to right, until they dropped and Mortimer could tell that Violet had disappeared from view. Fuddle turned back to Mortimer.

"Oh, I like them all," he said absently.

Mortimer produced *Tragic Kingdom*.

"May I recommend this to you?" Mortimer asked. "It's a remarkable album. It was written by a young woman while she was in the throes of a breakup with her boyfriend of seven years. It's bitter and honest. Madonna is good, but I think you might find that this album has an openness that really speaks to you."

Mortimer concluded, "It is my favorite album in the world."

Fuddle looked at Mortimer for a moment. He still looked lost. His hand gripped the Madonna CD as it had held the flowers moments ago. He finally composed himself and managed a smile as he started for the cash register.

"Thanks," he said, raising the disc a little so that Mortimer could see. "This is better."

26.

The Bavarian concessionaire Anton Feuchtwanger brought the hot dog bun to America in 1904. That year, he sold hot dogs at the Louisiana Purchase Exposition in St. Louis, piping hot frankfurters that burned to the touch. As a courtesy, Feuchtwanger loaned white gloves to the patrons to hold the sausages, but the customers did not return the favor and the gloves steadily disappeared. This was a cost Feuchtwanger could not afford to absorb. He turned for help to his brother-in-law, a baker, who came up with the cheap and disposable idea of a warm folded bun, which continues, of course, to be used to this day.

In those days, meat vendors sold frankfurters individually or in strips, as sausages are sold in many modern butcher stores. By the early 1940s, though, hot dogs had become so popular that manufacturers began to package them in plastic, ten to a pack, ready for sale. The number ten had no special significance to it. One of the early hot dog distributors chose it arbitrarily, but it soon acquired enough momentum to become the industry standard.

Around the same time, bakers began mass marketing sandwich rolls, for which demand ran high, as people needed buns for the frankfurters that they consumed in ever-increasing numbers. The bakers sold them eight to a pack. The number eight had no special significance to it. Bakers traditionally cooked in eight-roll pans, but they could have chosen any size pan they wanted for the new product. They chose the number eight merely for its familiarity, but it soon gathered enough momentum to become the industry standard.

This disparity inconvenienced patrons, who had to purchase hot dogs and buns in multiples of forty if they did not want to have any left over after their barbecues. This did not inhibit sales, as people would have their hot dogs and buns one way or the other, but it left customers grumbling in the supermarket aisles, which undermined the considerable good will for frankfurters and rolls. Both the hot dog and bun manufacturers understood that something needed to be done.

In 1952, representatives of the two camps met at the Bretton Woods Lodge in the foothills of the White Mountains to try and negotiate a solution. In honor of the occasion, the hotel served hot dogs on buns morning, noon, and night. This came at the suggestion of the industry leaders, but as the days went by it began to wear on the conferees. Some would have liked another type of sausage with their breakfast, or to have had their eggs with a bagel instead of a bun, or just to have had a nice bowl of cereal. They would have even settled for divorcing the two occasionally, so that they didn't have to eat their plate of franks and beans in the evening with bits of bun crumbled into the stew. But politics demanded otherwise. So the conferees smiled, and ate their hot dogs and rolls day after day, their patience growing thin.

They made little progress.

The hot dog people felt strongly about their position. They could not say exactly why. No one remembered how frankfurters came to be sold ten to a pack. And it would not have taken much to change, just an order to cut the plastic seal in different size strips. But all the same, it seemed important to the hot dog people to protect their interests. Things had been done this way for more than a decade. They were disinclined to change. And, after all, they made the meat, and what was a hot dog bun without a hot dog?

At the same time, the bun people felt strongly about their own position, though they could not say exactly why either. No one remembered why rolls came eight to a pack. And it would not have taken much to change, just a minimal investment in some new pans. But all the same it seemed important to the bun people to protect their interests. Generations of bakers had used pans of eight. They were disinclined to change. And they did not appreciate the condescension of the hot dog people, parading around as if they owned the world because people liked their sausages. Everyone knew they were mostly filler. And, after all, where would the hot dog be without the bun?

So the two sides went back and forth, sitting across the same table day after day, making the same arguments, and eating hot dogs and buns disguised in as many ways as the hotel chef could think of. Sometimes one party or the other would tout a creative solution to the problem, but these were inevitably simply more veiled ways of asking the other side to capitulate. No middle ground was to be had. One side or the other had to give, though each would have benefited from an agreement whether they were the party that capitulated or not. In this case, being magnanimous had no cost. Each side understood this. Each side understood they had it within their own power to improve things for everyone. And yet they could not agree.

There were times when the leaders of each side thought to themselves that they would chime in and say that they would be the bigger man and absorb the cost of the change. And each time they held their tongue, for reasons they did not understand themselves. It was as if they couldn't help themselves.

In the end the two sides parted ways, friendly but not friends, a wary eye turned over their respective shoulders towards the other. Each side blamed the other. Amongst themselves the hot dog men called the bun people stubborn and simple-minded. In turn their adversaries called them arrogant and rigid. But the truth was simpler: they could not rise above themselves.

Which meant that no one got what they wanted.

27.

One night Mortimer wandered to the river, downstream from where he usually ran, away from the bums and the feral dogs, and sat upon a solitary bench between the Cloisters Museum and the water. The summer had started to melt away, and the cool night air hinted of autumn. It felt good on his skin, refreshing and clean.

He soon fell into a deep and dreamless sleep, the sort of sleep he had not had in years, the sleep of a child. He awoke disoriented. It seemed that days had passed. He did not know where he was. Then he heard the soft rippling of the waters of the Hudson River. The familiar sights of the George Washington Bridge and the lights of Hoboken called to him. He came back.

It all seemed strange to him. Years ago, before he unsuccessfully overdosed on stool softener, Mortimer had come to this river with the thought of drowning himself. Back then he had everything: youth, intelligence, access to the finest education in the world. He held his fate in his hands, a career in science or math or anything he chose. And all he could think of then was to tie a stone around his ankles and sink himself to the bottom of the filthy river. Today, in comparison, he had nothing, but he could not fathom the thought of abandoning his life.

Mortimer watched the river flow with fascination. He heard its voice clearly. He heard many things now that he had never heard before, the sound of his own mind, the sounds of life. He had opened his soul to all kinds of new experiences and sensations. The voice of the river held special appeal for him. It captivated him, enticing him like the song of the Sirens. The river seemed to have something to tell him, something strange and wonderful, something he did not know.

Mortimer sat still and let it come to him. Life worked best when allowed to approach at its own pace.

In the distance he saw a boy on a bicycle. The boy seemed to be working. He would pedal for a few yards, then stop and dismount and post something on the side of one of the lampposts that lined the river. As he came nearer, Mortimer began to hear the voice of the river more clearly. It seemed to say *pay heed, pay heed*. It spoke elegantly, and with good grammar.

The boy pedaled up at his leisurely pace, rested his bicycle against the rail, taped a sign to the base of the lamp, then went on his way up the river. When the boy had finished, Mortimer rose from the bench to see what he had posted.

The sign said:

NO DOUBT

ROCK STEADY TOUR

BEACON THEATER

DECEMBER 18-20

Mortimer smiled at the river. His old life had ended. His life of transitory pleasures and material possessions lied behind him. Now he had been given a chance for something permanent and sublime.

And he was prepared.

28.

From the journal of Mortimer Taylor Coleridge

Waiting.

    Alive!

29.

Without looking up, Mortimer knew she had entered the store. The hair on the back of his neck stood up as if he had started the ascent up a roller coaster. His skin tingled. Blood rushed to his head; he felt flush and heavy. His stomach fluttered and his left knee buckled.

He began breathing deeply, in and out, over and over, relying upon his training to steady himself. The casual observer would not have noticed the subtle change in his breath. Months of practice had honed his ability to reap the benefits of this act without any perceptible alteration in his appearance. Soon it began to have the desired effect. Oxygen flooded his body. He chanted to himself: *Om. Om. Om.* His mind cleared.

"One with sauerkraut."

He turned his focus to his work. With a wave of his hand, the dressing was loaded. Quarter in hand, he produced the frankfurter. Then, steadying himself with one last breath, he looked up from the counter.

It was she.

She was more beautiful than she looked on television and in videos, more beautiful than he had ever dreamed. There she was made up, which was nice; she looked wonderful like that too.

But this was the real thing, which was so much better. She had such a natural beauty: soft, beautiful skin, puffy red lips. An aura engulfed her. She did not seem to be of this planet, just an angel down visiting for the day.

She was fifth in line, four people away.

Mortimer continued taking orders. "One Gutbuster with sauerkraut and mustard." He felt conscious of his movements; his fingers, lithe and nimble, danced through the order. One with kraut and mustard. Two with kraut and mustard. Three.

Was she watching?

He breathed and chanted. *Om. Om. Om.*

"One with sauerkraut."

He thought about taking another look at her. He had not allowed himself this in his planning—it was important that she not notice him staring at her. Surely, however, she had not noticed him the first time. It was too hard to resist. He glanced up as he produced the order.

She was still there.

Two to go.

"Two with mustard and sauerkraut. One plain, one with mustard, two with mustard and sauerkraut to go."

Mortimer didn't hear a word of it. In ten years, he had never had such a lapse of concentration. A bit ashamed, he looked up at the customer. She had a baby hanging from her neck.

"I'm sorry," he said.

"What are you sorry about?"

"I didn't hear the order."

The customer repeated it, peeved.

"So that's four with mustard and sauerkraut?"

"What didn't you understand? It's two with mustard and sauerkraut. Then four to go, one plain, one with mustard, two with mustard and sauerkraut."

"Right, so that's a total of four with mustard and sauerkraut."

"Let me be clear." She condescended to him now, speaking slowly as if he were unable to understand English spoken at normal speed. "Six total. Two to stay, four to go. The two to stay take mustard and sauerkraut. One of the to-goes is plain, one takes mustard; the others get mustard and sauerkraut. Can you do that?"

Mortimer seethed. She hadn't said the plain one and the one with mustard were to go before. This created the ambiguity that he had tried to clear up. It was her fault, not his. She spoke to him as if he were an idiot, but she was the idiot. And for her to try to show him up, now of all times, took more gall than could be comprehended. He drew his breath to put the woman in her place. Then his training kicked in. He held his tongue and calculated the potential consequences.

Would sympathy run in his favor or hers? He worried that Gwen would think him stupid based on the exchange, but would she? Would she look unfavorably upon him for being slow or disdain the woman for holding up the line with such a difficult order? The woman had ordered imprecisely. Anyone could see that. And no good could come out of snapping back at the woman. The customer was always right. He might even score points for being gracious to such a boorish patron.

Mortimer produced the hot dogs without a word. The woman took them with a grunt and went on her way. He then stole another glance at Gwen. Risky, but he had to know. She did not appear to have noticed any of it. She was reading one of the signs, Mortimer's favorite as it was. It said:

Life is Short

"Be Happy"

Mortimer smiled to himself. His training had saved him. The study, hard work, and sacrifice had all been worth it.

"Two with mustard and sauerkraut."

Mortimer's confidence surged. He breezed through the order. The frankfurters were dressed in a moment, the condiments appearing as if they had been conjured by prestidigitation. The customer watched in awe as Mortimer worked, shaking his head in amazement when two quarters appeared in his hand in the same motion that the two dollar bills were taken away. He had just seen a master at work.

Mortimer felt full of himself, centered. All of his doubts slipped from his mind; his deepest questions had been answered. Once he had despaired because life seemed to have no meaning. We have no control over any of it, the notion of free will nothing more than an illusion created by man himself to make the misery more palatable. The things that we believe make us distinct, that set us apart from animals, are all myths. We are all the same, all servants to the same master, a persistent and tireless taskmaster with a mind for only one thing: to live for the sake of living. It sets its legion of marionettes dancing to further this arbitrary end, life perpetuating life for no discernable reason. None of it means anything.

So he once believed.

Now these insidious notions faded from his mind like vapors to the wind. He saw his error now. He found the meaning in it all. He understood. His entire life had been directed to this moment. Everything that came before had been prologue, a tortured path with twists and turns, but always steering him towards this destination. He could not see it at times, but it had been there always. The hard times, the disgrace, the suffering of fools, all of it had been to prepare him for this instant. An invisible hand guiding him to his destiny. One could not deny the presence of such a force at work. The supporting evidence overwhelmed.

He was there. She was there. It could not be more clear.

He had been wrong, too, to believe that nothing set man apart. One thing did, and that was love. Not the puppy love of teenagers or the peccadilloes of middle age. These fancies faded; they were no different than what passes between swans. But another matter entirely was transcendent love, the kind of love that can only pass between thoughtful men and women, men and women who have suffered, the kind that lasts forever. This was the kind he meant. This made man different. He saw this now too.

He opened his heart. He was prepared, ready.

She stepped up to the counter.

He made full eye contact with her, to let her know that he

knew who she was, but that he was not intimidated. Her eyes met his; they locked. For how long? A second? A lifetime? It made no difference. The point had been made. He felt the force between them. He knew she felt it too.

Mortimer parted his lips. These would be the first words between them, the first of a lifetime of words. His destiny had arrived.

"Can I help you?"

Mortimer flinched. Being ungrammatical had not been part of the plan. If she knew him better, she might recognize it as a colloquialism. She might even appreciate that he remained unaffected despite his exemplary schooling. But she did not have this background. She would think him dim, ordinary. He corrected himself.

"I mean *may* I help you."

She smiled. Was she smiling in appreciation of his good form or because she thought him some silly sycophant? He had no time to consider the question. It was most important now that he not appear flustered.

He said nothing more.

She said, "Two plain, please." Just as he had anticipated: no foul spices or soured cabbage to spoil the plain goodness of the meat. She ordered them just as he liked them himself. It was a bond, their first. He felt aglow.

Mortimer's fingers reached for the bun warmer, as they had a million times before. He tilted the stainless steel door with his left hand as he reached down with his right to pull two buns from the crisper. His senses were at their most acute. He smelled the wafting aroma of the bun, felt its moistness and warmth against his calloused fingers. He heard the sounds of the crowd. His heightened sensitivities allowed him to single out conversations, to pick out individual voices. Or he could retreat into himself and hear the sounds of everything at once. This is what he did. He listened to the cacophonous amalgam, the collective din of the sounds of life.

He was alive.

With a sweep of his hand, Mortimer began his signature move, a flip of the bun from his right hand to his left—it would turn twice, end over end—as he reached with his right hand to spear the hot dog. When the bun landed on the counter the frankfurter would be waiting. He felt a sense of a calm as he went into the motion, the confidence of an actor that has rehearsed his role for a lifetime.

He flipped the bun.

From the moment it left his hand he knew something was wrong. He did not feel the familiar snap of his wrist. The bun did not rotate, end over end, as it usually did. It went straight up in the air, not very high, and landed far off the mark, on the side of the counter, near Mortimer's right elbow, where he could not reach it. It dangled there on the edge. For a second, Mortimer thought it might manage to hold on, but too much of its weight had shifted to the outside. It fell to the floor, landing with a pathetic thud.

Mortimer smiled. This had not been part of the plan either.

He needed to set things right. He reached down and pulled out another bun. Again he flipped it from his right hand to his left, making sure to put adequate force behind it this time. Instead, he used too much, and it sailed over his left shoulder, striking the sign behind Mortimer's station, the one that said:

"We Use the Freshest Ingredients"

Panic surged through his body. When the errant bun landed, he turned to her. She showed no signs of perturbation. She waited patiently, indulging him. No doubt she thought him some tyro, dallying at the hot dog arts, out to impress the celebrity with some feat of *machismo*, which he had not adequately practiced. No doubt.

He needed to correct that misimpression, needed to explain to her that he was not some amateur, some johnny-come-lately; that he was a master artisan.

The words sounded pathetic as they came out, and he wanted to pull them back as soon as they passed his lips.

"I've been doing this for ten years," he said.

She smiled. "The best hot dog in the world," she said. A giant sign on the front window declared this same point. It had a citation at the end of the quote—from *Consumer Reports*—but who could say whether one food was better than another? It was all a matter of taste. Had she been mocking the sign? This thought pleased him, but had she been mocking him at the same time, aping a mantra she believed he would credit while smiling knowingly to herself all the while? Was she patronizing him? Was she taking him seriously?

Mortimer retrieved another bun from the crisper, this time placing it down directly on the counter, no flipping. He reached with his tongs to lift a frankfurter from the grill. He approached this task conservatively, too. He would not grab multiple hot dogs, as he usually did. He would take one at a time and set each carefully upon its bun. He squeezed the utensil and lifted; it glided above the counter, the meat secure in its clutches. He squeezed too hard, though. Perhaps it was nerves, perhaps it was the small pool of sweat that had formed in the palm of his hand. Whatever the reason, he held on too tightly. The frankfurter spurted out. It took a short flight before striking the glass panel in front of his station, then collapsing pathetically on the counter, flaccid.

Mortimer sheepishly turned his eyes upward; his mind raced for words. They surprised him as much as anyone when they spilled out.

"The harder I push the tension does grow."

The line came from a song called "The Climb" from the *Tragic Kingdom* album. It told the story of an arduous ascent up a mountain: "So high the climb/Can't turn back now/Must keep climbing up to the clouds." It might perhaps be interpreted as a metaphor for something deeper—careers, life—but Mortimer didn't think so. He thought it was just about a hike up a hill. It wasn't one of the band's better songs. Her brother wrote it. It hadn't received much play. Mortimer wondered whether she even remembered the lyric.

She smiled politely.

"Take your time," she said.

Mortimer could not have felt smaller. She thought him simple, pathetic. He cursed himself. He wanted to burst out of his skin so his spirit could be free of this useless body, so she could see him for his true self, a soaring eagle among men.

He speared another hot dog and placed it upon the bun, then another. He felt calmer now. He had made so many mistakes that he had nothing left to prove. He placed each of the hot dogs in their paper cradles—she had not indicated whether she wanted them to go—and lifted them to the serving counter.

His mind raced. Time was running out. Soon the moment would be gone. What could he do? What could he do?

He relied on his training. He breathed deeply one last time, which cleared his mind. He remembered his original plan. It could still work; it might even work better. The words would have even more meaning given everything that had happened. He felt a rush of optimism as he set the hot dogs down and drew his breath again. This could change it all. This would change it all.

"Look at me," he said. "I'm a person."

He didn't quite say it the way he imagined it, though. His mouth had become dry. The words came out more as a mumble than anything else; the first few words of each sentence were barely audible. It ended up sounding like "Me... person."

She smiled again, took the hot dogs and handed Mortimer her money. She had exact change: a dollar fifty. Mortimer returned the fifty cents he had palmed to the cash register.

"Thank you," she said.

"Welcome," said Mortimer. He had intended this to be prefaced by "you're," but the contraction failed to make it out of his mouth.

She walked out. A head or two turned. Some people recognized her, some didn't. Some cared, some didn't. A few of the employees knew who it was. Garcia went in and pulled Bertrand Fuddle out of his office. He thought it would be good for Fuddle since the manager had been in the cramped room all day without saying a word. Fuddle came out reluctantly. He stood in the doorway and watched for a moment, bewildered at the commotion. When she left he stepped back into his office without a word and returned to his misery and the business of counting buns.

Soon everyone returned to their business. The countermen resumed selling hot dogs. The customers took up whatever conversation they had paused. The students standing at the counter picked up their books and began studying chemistry and philosophy again. Already their brains had set in motion the process that would turn the event into the collection of chemicals and electrical impulses called a memory. For them it had been only a moment's distraction.

Life went on.

Mortimer nodded his head to one of his colleagues; the boy stepped up to relieve him. Mortimer then loosened his apron and hung it on the hook outside of Fuddle's office. Then he pushed his way through the crowd and walked out to the street.

It was a brilliant day in the city, the summer flaunted its

ebbing but still considerable power. Mortimer squinted in the sun. He had been inside Papaya Queen for too long, and his eyes had grown accustomed to the dim fluorescent lighting.

He scanned the streets, looking for her. People scattered in every direction: mothers pushing babies in carriages, friends chatting away the day, solitary figures contemplating the world. Some were on the way to the Papaya Queen for hot dogs; some had just eaten there. Some were going shopping, some to the Xerox store to copy important documents, some to the cobbler to have their shoes mended. Some were in a rush, some took their time. Some seemed anxious, some content. Some were absorbed in themselves, others took in the goings-on. Mortimer could focus in on any one of them if he wanted, telescope his sights and wonder what went through his mind or hers, what made this one tick, what pushed that one's buttons. Or he could draw back and take it all in at once, a mosaic of color and movement, a rivulet in the sea of humanity. Life.

He called out to her. His voice had returned to him, too late. He spoke the name gently, with desperation, a final plea to the heavens. The word felt soft on his lips.

"Gwen."

But it was too late. She was gone.

CHORUS

Perhaps people like us cannot love. Ordinary people can—that is their secret.

– Siddartha

From the journal of Mortimer Taylor Coleridge

You think you're better than me, I know.

If you're reading this it means you've taken some time from your busy lives, time from your fruit tarts and your pudding snacks, from your carpools and your commuter trains, from your recliner chairs and your chin-up bars. It means you've taken time from all of these important things to read these pages filled with my ruminations, to take this peek into my life and to reflect upon what it says about your own existence.

I know what you're feeling right now: pity, empathy, contempt. Some of one, a little of the other, more derision from the less generous among you, greater compassion from those more charitably inclined. But through all of you, the munificent and miserly alike, beats the same overwhelming sentiment, drumming like a cadence: I'm better than that. I'm better than that.

How sad, you say, to squander such a promising career and such a fertile mind. He would have been a fine geneticist, you say. He had all the tools. And heaven knows the world could use a few good ones. Has there been a truly great geneticist since Gregor Mendel?

Or if not a geneticist, then a writer perhaps. He has such a clever wit and expressive voice. Perhaps a writer who writes about genetics. Something. Anything. He had too much talent to waste it all working in a hot dog stand.

And then this thing with the rock star. How pitiful. Even after all of it—after dropping out of Columbia and the breakdown, or whatever it was—he still had a chance to be happy. The girl seemed nice enough. What was her name, Viola, Victoria? Maybe she was nothing special, but then again he was nothing special either. And she seemed to really care for him. He should have counted himself lucky. He could have had a life with her, kids, a nice apartment, maybe even a house someday. And then he throws it all away for some rock star he sees in a video.

It was an impetuous and unbalanced reaction. Nothing about it makes any sense. He didn't know anything about her. So she wrote a few songs that appealed to him. So she gave a few interviews that suggested she might be a thoughtful and emotionally honest person. What does any of this mean? This is just her public persona, an image constructed by advertising executives and video producers. It has nothing to do with who she really is.

And even if he were right, even if she were the sweetest, most decent person in the world, and he were the single human being who could make her most happy, her simpatico, her soul mate, what then? How exactly would this all have worked out? Suppose he had caught her eye that day. Suppose that instead of fumbling with the frankfurter and stammering like a dolt he had said something profound. Then what? Did he really think a rock star from California would go for a hot dog vendor, especially one with an immense ingrown hair on his cheek? It's so sad to think that he thought that. Pathetic really.

And sadder still is his entire outlook on life, this notion that choice is an illusion, that we are programmed to behave in a certain way, that we can't rise above any of it. The saddest part of the whole story is that he had the instruments of his own happiness at his disposal: the girl, a career, a keen intellect. He had it all there at his fingertips had he chosen to take any of it and instead he told himself that he didn't have a choice at all, that things couldn't have been any other way.

I know what you're saying: that's the saddest part of the story. That's what's really pathetic.

You think you're better than I am, better than all of this.

You would never have lost it in the first place. And especially not over philosophy or biology or something some cranky old professor said in class. These are just words. You would never lose it over that.

And if you did lose it you would get it back together and surely rise to something better than working in a hot dog stand. And if it had to be a hot dog stand then you would make the best of that, too. If you were lucky enough to find a girl like Violet, you'd grab onto her with both hands and never let go, certainly not for some singer you saw on MTV or VH1 or whatever it was. You'd never let yourself fall for her.

Even if you did fall for her, you would not let it ruin your life. You'd have kept it in the back of your mind. Maybe you'd go see one of their shows. Maybe you'd buy some magazine with a spread of pictures of her or a poster. Nothing more than that. You would never throw it all away for her. You would never toss aside your life for some surge of lust-inducing hormones. You would never do any of that.

And most of all, if you did any of it or all of it you would never allow yourself the luxury, the convenience, of telling yourself that it was all anything other than a choice. You would own up to it. You control your own life. You are its master.

You would never do such a thing. You are better than this.

Are you sure?

Do you know?

When a pretty man or woman walks down the street do you let him or her go by unnoticed? Or do you look? Before you know it do you find that you have craned your neck and passed a moment wondering what it might be like to bed the person, wondering without any act of volition, a powerless victim of your hormonal cravings?

Are you ever jealous? Do you ever wonder what it might be like to inhabit someone else's body, to know the pleasures he knows, to look as she looks? Are you above all this? Or do you find yourself staring, even if you have more than anyone could ever dream to have, staring like Gwen:

I wish I looked exactly like her
What's it like to have that body?
I'm gawking while I wonder

Do you still want the bad boyfriend, even while the gentle suitor beckons at your elbow, ready to cater to your whim? Do you lust for the man or woman you cannot possess, no matter who he or she is, no matter who you already have? Do you covet membership to the club that will not have you? Do you want the bigger car, the bigger house, what she fancies, what he has?

When you watch a soap opera or a maudlin love story, do you shake your head in derision or do you find yourself yearning for more: for the moonlight strolls on the beach, for the staggeringly handsome man who sees stars when he looks in your eyes, for the happy ending?

Do you see yourself in movies? In rock videos? In adventure stories? Do you say to yourself: This is not real. Or do you think: that could be me? That should be me.

Are you content with what you have? Or do you still want it all?

When bad things happen to you do you place them in context, as people tell you to do, as your rational mind suggests you should, or do you wallow in self-pity? Do you think about the children in Somalia who wonder where their next meal will come from, who grow up without shoes on their feet or a roof over their heads, and give thanks for your own good fortune? When bad things happen do you think about them, as you know you should, or do you think only of your own plight? How could this have happened to me? It is the end of the world.

Can you turn your emotions on and off, like a faucet?

Do you possess exquisite self-control?

Are you the master of your life?

Do you fancy yourself in command? Or do you sometimes

wonder who is at the helm of your own ship? Do you ever say to yourself, "This is not what I chose?" Do you ever wonder, "How have I gotten here?" In your most private moments—in your office daydreams, your rush hour broods, your bedroom fantasies—do you sometimes feel yourself awash in the current? Do you find yourself repeating the same patterns, new faces and places, but the same old reactions and the same old feelings? Do you ever wonder if you can break free? Do you ever feel it all spinning out of control?

You think you are the master of your life.

You think you're better than I am.

Are you sure?

Do you know?